SKATE

A NOVEL BY

Stephen E. Meyer

ISBN (Print): 978-1-09837-828-8
ISBN (eBook): 978-1-09837-829-5

Contents

MAP #1

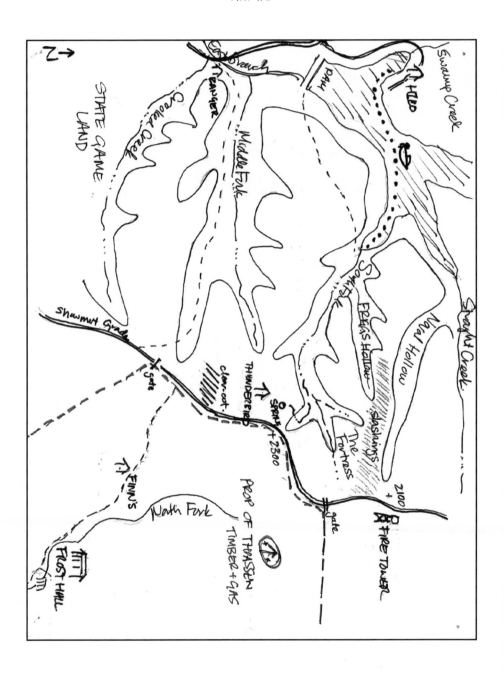

MAP #2

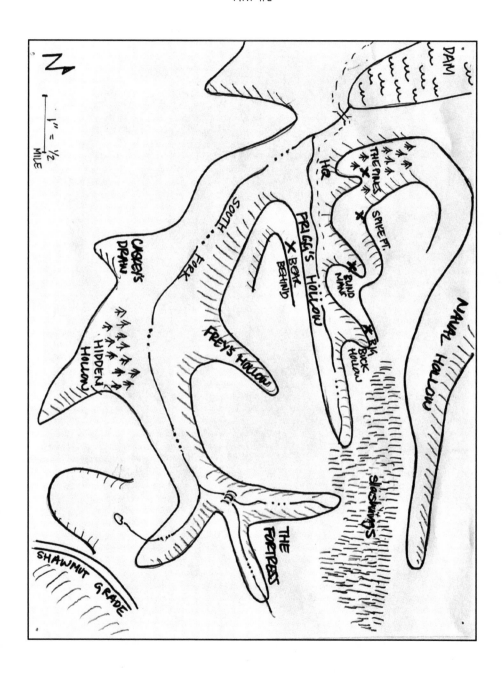

A NOTE TO THE READER

The events in this story happened in the late 1980s—just before the rise of the Internet—which will help explain why characters don't google things, use apps, carry phones, or send texts.

PRELUDE

Looking down from space at night, there's a dark patch, a hole in the tapestry of lights that outline the East Coast—a bypassed place where the map edges don't line up and easier to go around. Even the glaciers stopped shy of this high plateau, where the land tilts upward in a flat slope then ruptures through the earth like a giant's fist, topped with knuckled ridges and deeply creased hollows.

Centuries ago, the Seneca Nation, who lived on the northern edge, generally avoided the area—a gloomy upland forest of ancient hemlocks and swamps, so dense the sun barely reached the ground, blanketed with heavy lake-effect snows in the winter. There were a few hunting trails for whitetailed deer and the elk that hid in the bogs.

The first white settlers were late to arrive, a bunch of rubes, fresh off the boat, fooled by pamphlets showing a rolling expanse of farmland with sailing schooners plying wide rivers, easily tricked by Philadelphia lawyers into signing quitclaim deeds. They arrived in the dead of winter, in a blizzard, built a chapel among the pines, and barely survived until spring. Even though this was virgin country, no one followed after them. While they struggled in the snow, gold had been discovered in California.

The first thing they did was cut down all of the trees. Tram roads were etched into hillsides, penetrating further and further into the forest. The tree rings revealed hemlocks that were over five hundred years old. Logs were floated downriver to sawmills, the bark used for tanning hides into leather in stinking vats on the edge of town, and a paper mill was established and belched noxious steam into the skies. The last elk was killed, its head mounted on display in the county courthouse.

Then a new gold rush occurred—black gold. Rock oil found seeping out of the ground into streams led to the first wells being drilled, and soon the center of the world's oil production was here. Little boomtowns popped up, with a rush of immigrants from Germany, Ireland, Slovakia, and Scandinavia. Railroads snaked down the long river valleys to suck oil away.

Soon the oil industry moved on to richer, more productive fields in Texas and Oklahoma leaving behind derricks to rust in the snow. But a new demand arose from steel mills in Pittsburgh, hungry for the coal that lay underneath the ridge tops. The old logging roads were turned into short-track railroads, creeping up into hollows to cart away coal to feed the blast furnaces.

The hunger was so great, production from these lonely mine shafts dotting the backwoods wasn't enough. New techniques were devised, *with heavy machines, to strip off entire hilltops and lay open the seams of coal. The runoff from these mines turned the streams orange and sulphurous. By now the old-growth forest was gone, nothing left but bare, muddy hillsides and thick briar patches for miles and miles.*

And then it all came to an end. Cheaper sources of coal were obtained from enormous open-pit mines out West. Two World Wars and the Great Depression siphoned away generations of men and few returned to this forgotten corner, finding easier work in the big cities and suburbs instead. The railroads stopped running, replaced by interstate highways with trucks and cars that avoided these mountains altogether. Boomtowns became ghost towns.

Left alone, the forest slowly returned, but it was a different forest than the ancient hemlocks. From the briar patches grew oaks and maples, chestnut and beech, black cherry and ironwood. Caught up in the conservation movement, enormous tracts of land were declared state game lands and national forests. Deer flourished. The streams ran clear again and trout were stocked. Elk were transported from the Rockies. In time, the place became known as a sportsman's paradise, not too far a drive from Pittsburgh or Philadelphia, but far enough that few moved permanently. Hunting camps were established out in the woods, little more than shacks that stood empty most of the year, except for the weekend after Thanksgiving when smoke appeared in chimneys and trucks parked out front, preparing for the first day of deer season.

FRIDAY

Stef Yeager steered his old man's pickup truck along the muddy road, swerving to miss the crater-sized potholes, jerking the wheel back to avoid skidding off the side of the narrow track. There were steep banks along either side, a built-up embankment on the left and cliff-like slopes on the right. This dirt road used to be the Shawmut Grade, the old railroad that traced along the crest of the eastern continental divide, but had been abandoned decades ago, the iron rails and wooden ties long since removed. The low sun winked through the bare trees on the ridgeline and cast long shadows down the hollows. He couldn't help but steal a glance up at the hills as he drove, looking to see if he might spot some deer.

About ten miles outside of town, a black iron gate crossed the road. It was shaped like a capital A turned on its side, with an old tire lashed in the center like a big letter O. Covering the tire on the side facing him was a logo, a circle with an upward-pointing arrow painted in the middle, and two stars, one on each side. A big yellow sign read "Posted. Property of Thiassen Timber & Gas. Hunting, fishing, trapping, or trespassing for any purpose is strictly prohibited."

Stef parked the truck and got out, ducked underneath the gate and walked about ten yards off the side of the road, to the base of a big oak tree, where there was a rusted coffee can among the fallen acorns. He shook it and heard the rattle inside. Just where his old man said it would be.

The gate was counterbalanced by a paint bucket filled with concrete, weighted so it naturally swung open in a wide, lazy arc, almost grazing the front grill of the parked truck, until the tire banged into an iron post planted just-so on the side of the road and rattled to a stop there.

Before getting back into the truck, Stef went over to the edge of the road and pissed off the west side, where the streams fed the Clarion, the Allegheny, the Ohio, the Mississippi, and down to the Gulf of Mexico. It took some skill to stop mid-stream, waddle across the road, and resume on the other side of the divide, which drained into the Sinnemahoning, the Susquehanna, the Chesapeake, and then the Atlantic. One leak, ending up thousands of miles apart.

He drove the truck through, hopped out and shut the gate behind him, and continued on. To the right, a small side-road plunged straight down into the cavernous valley of North Fork, at the bottom of which stood Frost Hall, the Thiassen hunting lodge. Everything to the east of the road was owned by the company and posted with yellow signs, plus they owned this gated section of the road itself. Everything to the west was state game lands, open to the public, but because there was no other access to this land it meant, in addition to the thousand acres they owned outright, this stretch of woods was in essence Thiassen's private hunting ground as well.

Stef had never been to Frost Hall, but his old man had, and told him of the legendary trophy bucks mounted in the main hall. Rich people flew into the little airport outside of town for the weekend with private guides and trails blazed to all of the best spots.

After another mile he passed a food plot, land cleared by the game commission and planted with feed for deer: grass, clover, or— in the case of this field—turnips, their leafy green tops standing out vividly against the drab brown November background with glimpses of purple peeking through the dirt. At the edge of the plot were big mesh tumblers filled with corn. A bit of a joke, putting food plots way out here, all they did was fatten up the deer for the out-of-state hunters down at Frost Hall. Thiassen had certainly made a contribution to the game commision along the way.

At last he came to a clearing, a south-facing meadow filled with tall indian grass, goldenrods no longer yellow but with fuzzy gray tips, milkweed with burst pods, and purple briar-bushes grown up around the fringes. The woods beyond were recently clear-cut, all but a few trees remaining, marked with blue spray-painted Xs. A fresh gouge of mud showed the ruts of the tires where the logging trucks had gone in. At the boundary of the meadow where the clear-cut began was a turnaround and a pile of cut logs, marked with a strip of red plastic tied in a bow on a branch.

He parked, got out, stretched, and cast a glance at the sun. About noon, though it was hard to believe with the sun hanging so low in the sky. He looked at the woodpile. It had seemed an ordinary job when his old man said, "Go out the grade and fill up the truck with firewood for the camp." But now faced with it, the size of the logs that needed to be split—big around as his arms—and how big the flatbed of the truck was, Stef let out a deep sigh. *Better get to it.*

He picked out the widest, flattest log section he was able to pry loose from the pile and rolled it out to a level spot of ground to serve as a chopping block. Then he carried over a log from the top of the pile, cut crisp on both ends and almost a perfect cylinder, and propped it so it stood vertically on top of the chopping block. From the back of the truck he took the five-pound maul, a rusted iron wedge in case he needed it, and a pair of work gloves.

He rolled up the cuffs of his flannel shirt and pushed up his long underwear sleeves and hefted the maul, his right hand cupping the neck near the axe-head and the other at the base of the wooden handle, set his legs at an angle with the weight resting on his thigh, and then rocked his hips back to set it in motion, lifted his arms up high, swinging the maul in an arc above his head, stepping forward and squaring his hips as he brought the blade down. *THUNK*—the swing struck the log off-center, blunting the force of the blow, sending an ache up through his hands and shoulders, and causing the log to tumble end over end off the chopping block, intact.

He swore.

Immediately frustrated, he retrieved the log, jammed it back on top of the block where it wobbled a little then stood straight. Once again, he took a deep breath, focused, and let his anger brush away any other thoughts as he took another big swing. *CRACK*—the axe head split clean through and bit into the chopping block below. The two of the log halves dropped onto the ground on opposite sides with satisfying soft thuds, revealing the orange—almost pink—woodgrain inside.

Black cherry. Exceedingly rare, only really found in these mountains, magically appearing after the old growth forest was cut down a century ago. Lumber from these trees went for a fortune, was prized for furniture and cabinets. *Hard to believe they left behind a pile like this to be split for firewood.*

He shrugged—this was nothing new for his old man, a well-known lawyer in town who did legal work like wills and deeds for all kinds of people, families that knew his grandpa and further back, and some of them paid their bills with barter, like the farmers who brought the Thanksgiving turkey each year in return for having their taxes done. This was the same thing, though he didn't have a clue what the old man had done for Thiassen. It seemed like they had plenty of cash on hand and didn't need to pay in firewood.

Back to it. He started to work himself into a good rhythm—get a log from the pile, rotate it just right so it stood balanced on the chopping block, take the first big swing to bust it in half, then work on the halves, using a shorter sharper stroke to split into quarters, sometimes on the bigger logs, into sixths or eighths.

He was sweating, took off his flannel and tied it around his waist, went back and got one of the bigger sections, feeling invincible. Another swing and *THWOCK*—the axe head buried itself in the log, stuck. He had to kick at the handle to get the blade to pop out. *A knot.*

So, he took the iron wedge, placed it in the divot left by his first swing, flipped the maul head over to its flat end, and started to bang on it like a hammer. *CHINK … CHINK … CHINK.* Slowly the wedge worked down into the grain and the crack widened. He was breathing heavily, the maul suddenly felt twice its weight, his arms like lead taking the vibration of the metal directly in his joints. Finally, there was a popping and cracking sound as the knot unwound and the log twisted open into halves. The iron wedge clanked onto the ground.

He took a step back, looked at the firewood scattered on the ground around him—*Pretty decent amount.* Then he looked at the truck and the remaining pile, and then at the sun which didn't seem to have budged. There was a long way to go. He needed a break.

Back in the cab of the truck he got out the paper-bag lunch his mom had made for him, a turkey-and-stuffing sandwich from yesterday's leftovers, an apple, and a can of pop. He spotted something out in the field sticking up from the grass and walked over to investigate.

It was an old adirondack chair, weather-beaten and sagging. He eased himself down, grasping the arms of the chair, which was a little wobbly but sturdy enough to sit, leaned back and let out a sigh. The chair was situated on a little rise with a good view down across the meadow, through a gap in the tree line to the head end of Middle Fork hollow and the purple hilltops far to the west. *Good place to watch the sun set.* There were a couple of empty beer cans in the grass.

Stef chewed his sandwich, looked out at the landscape, and thought of nothing. The sun hit the chair directly and was just strong enough to generate warmth, and a very soft breeze dried his sweat. He closed his eyes and saw a pink glow behind his eyelids. He listened to the grass swish and fell fast asleep.

☙ ❧

From a deep sleep he became conscious of a steady crack-and-rattle sound, coming at regular intervals. It took a little while before he realized this was a real sound, from somewhere behind him, and a little while longer before he dragged himself awake, blinked his eyes open, and squinted into the sun.

He practically jumped out of the chair with a jolt. Right in front of him was a giant wolf–dog! It was less than five yards away, sitting on its hind legs, with its front legs upright, silver-white fur, pointed ears, panting with tongue lolling out of its mouth, yellow eyes fixed on him with a long stare.

His mind raced as he stared at the wolf–dog, a wave of pure adrenaline crashing through his blood, his heart pounding in his ears. *Could he move? Should he move?* And behind him, the cracking sound continued. Very subtly, the wolf–dog's eyes flicked away, focused beyond him. *What was back there?*

He quietly put pressure on the heel of his right hand and twisted his torso up and to the left, rotating his neck ever so slowly, keeping one eye on the wolf–dog while looking over his shoulder, trying to see behind the chair. Up by the chopping block there was a person—a woman—swinging an axe—*his axe!* —and busting up a log—*his log!* And then he continued twisting, a few degrees further in his arc of vision and stopped short—another wolf–dog, this one sitting a few feet directly behind him.

He let out a startled cry, "Aah!"

The sound of the chopping abruptly stopped, then came a short, sharp whistle. Both of the wolf-dogs immediately lost all interest in him and bounded up toward the woman.

"Heya!" she called out. "Sorry if these boys woke you!"

He stood bolt upright, stumbling a little, trying to compose himself. "N–no big deal. I must have dozed off!"

She stood with one bent elbow resting on a cocked hip, the axe at her side like an extension of her other arm, watching as he approached. She looked to be in her twenties and wore high-laced fur-lined boots, blue jeans, a zip-up fleece, and a blaze-orange kerchief that held back the long, ink-black hair from her face. She watched him with an even stare, the same expression as the two wolf–dogs at her side used. Though she was sweating heavily, her breathing was slow and measured.

"This your wood?" she asked.

He struggled for a response, still foggy from sleep. *The old man had cleared this with everyone, hadn't he?* He did not want to get in trouble trespassing, accused of stealing. But her tone wasn't challenging, it was matter-of-fact, almost bored.

"Yeah. I mean, it was left here for my dad? I'm just, you know, the one bringing it back."

She lifted her chin ever so slightly in acknowledgement, though he still couldn't read her response. *Why did she start cutting the firewood?* He glanced around. The ground circling the chopping block was filled with wedges, there must have been two-dozen logs busted up, and the main pile was practically gone. *How long was he asleep?!*

Finally, his manners caught up. "Thank you … for helping. I mean, wow. This is incredible."

She shrugged, nonchalant. "How about this. You get the wood loaded in the truck, I'll finish up the last few. Then you can give me a ride." It wasn't really phrased as a question.

He nodded, still a little dumbstruck. He got work gloves from his back pocket, the canvas firewood carrier from the truck bed, lowered the tailgate, then went and filled the U-shaped carrier until it was bulging, hauled it over to the truck with a kind of crab-walk, dumped the bag, and then returned for another load.

All the while, his mind was turning over. *What was she doing way out here … ten miles out of town … too far for an afternoon hike. And where did she want a ride to? And where would those giant dogs sit?* He watched them chasing each other around the meadow, tumbling like a pair of puppies except when one tired to nip at the other's neck with a flash of long white fangs. Not in the cab next to him. *No way.*

He watched her work fluidly, the start of each backswing lazy, pausing for a moment at the top of the swing arc, and then straight down, cleaving the wood so sharply that the big halves seemed to leap off the cutting board. When she worked on the half logs, she choked way up on the handle, held the five-pound maul like it was weightless, and sort of punched down on the log, each jab crisp and precise, moving rapidly in a semi-circle, *crack-crack-crack*, carving off smaller wedges without tipping the larger piece. Then, with a casual backhand, she flicked the final wedge off the block.

When she went to get the next log, he scurried in and filled up the carrier as quick as he could, not wanting to break her rhythm. Soon she was down to the last piece, a gnarly joint that looked like it held as many knots as knuckles in a fist.

He started, "You don't—" but she cut him short with a headshake.

Using the hammer end of the maul, she tapped the iron wedge into the surface, like getting a nail started. She stepped back, squared her hips, and slowly raised the maul above her head, her back and hips flexing, then with a mighty downward ringing blow, drove the wedge deep into the wood. She took another big swing. Another. Sparks flew from the clash of iron. And then striking with a low growl—the first time she made any sound of effort—the heart of the knot gave way and the log came asunder.

She made quick work of the pieces and soon they were done, the truck filled up with firewood. They leaned against the tailgate side by side in silence and looked out across the meadow. The late afternoon sun created a golden glow, the dogs sprawled out in the dry grass, napping.

"Want to grab a beer?" she asked him.

He was about to tell her his age and how he'd get carded at any bar in town, at the same time feeling a surge of pride that she took him for twenty-one. But before he could respond, she continued, "I'm staying about a mile further up the grade. You can give me a lift, maybe stop in for a minute."

Did she say further up the grade? There wasn't another thing out here in that direction for twenty miles, just state game land stretching in every direction. But before he could follow that train of thought any further, he caught her steady gaze, sky-blue eyes, at point-blank range.

"Sure," he said.

Then, after an awkward pause, "My name is Stef, by the way."

"Skate," she said, though at first he heard it as Kate, and only after a moment realized there was an *S* in front.

They shook hands, her hand clamping his like an iron vise. "Don't worry," she said, "the dogs can run alongside. They like chasing trucks." She flashed a dazzling grin.

❧

"Pull off here," she said. It looked like she was asking him to just drive straight into the woods. There was no side road on the left where she was pointing.

"Here," she said again, flatly. So he slowed down and eased the truck off the grade road and into the forest. Ahead, orange-brown leaves covered the ground. Suddenly he could see a way forward, more like an absence of trees rather than an actual defined path. He cautiously crept forward, the trees crowding in, some just inches away from the sides of the truck, a few low branches scraping against the roof.

They came over a slight rise and drove down into a bowl-shaped draw. In the center stood a little ramshackle hunting camp with clapboard siding, the wood black with age, a rusted corrugated tin roof, a stone chimney, and a few ill-fitting windows with cracked panes at the front and side. There was a Jeep parked alongside, otherwise he would swear the place was abandoned and had been for some time.

He pulled up next to the Jeep and they got out. Here in the dip the sun had dropped below the horizon, and while the tops of the trees glowed yellow, still catching rays, the camp and surroundings were cast in an inky gloom, the temperature suddenly about twenty degrees colder. He looked back, and couldn't see the main road from here. In fact, the path he had followed in was hard to make out.

"What is this place?" Stef said aloud, almost to himself.

"Old hunting camp," she said. "Been in the family, well, as far back as anyone cares to remember. No one comes here anymore, so I sort of claimed it." She put a finger up to her lips. "Shh. It's a secret." Then she laughed. "Come on, let's get a beer."

She walked around behind the camp and further down the draw, where there was a spring bubbling up from the ground, flowing over mossy stones and winding down into the head-end of a larger hollow just visible beyond. Alongside the spring was a single gnarled apple tree, totally out of place here in the forest, some golden apples still on the branches and many more scattered, withered and rotten, on the ground.

She noticed him looking at the tree and said, "Yeah, they were cheating." She pointed back at the camp. "The old timers would sit by the fire all day and if one came in they'd just lean out the window and 'Pow!' Easy drag."

She went over to the gurgling spring, pushed up a sleeve and plunged her hand into the black water, felt around, and came out with a six-pack of beer cans. Then she plucked a golden apple and took a crisp bite. "Want one?" she asked.

He shook his head no. She shrugged and headed back up toward the camp with him in tow. On their way around the far side was a well-worn footpath leading to an outhouse, and up against the side of camp stood a big cooler and a neatly stacked cord of firewood. She handed the six pack to him and he flinched at how icy-cold the cans were, making his knuckles instantly ache. She grabbed an armful of wood, the apple held clenched in her teeth, and nodded toward the front.

He went ahead and held the door open as she went inside, seeing the word "THUNDERBIRD" carved into the lintel above with a winged-bird car hood ornament mounted on top. A bunch of ancient license plates were hammered into the clapboard beside the entrance, as well as a big-dial thermometer.

He took a glance around before stepping through. The encircling woods were dead silent, the only sound the soft burbling of the spring. No sign of the dogs.

Inside was dim, with just the last bit of weak daylight filtering in through the windows. The camp was set up as a large single room, with a stone hearth and chimney centered on the opposite wall, a set of built-in bunks on the right hand side that could sleep six, maybe even twelve if two to a bed, and on the left a long wooden table with bench seating on either side. On the left wall were some pantry shelves, stacked with plates, cups, and dry goods, a counter and a basin sink, with milk jugs of water alongside. Two armchairs stood by the fireplace, which was smoldering with just a glint of orange coals. The roof was open to the rafters, with rack after rack of deer antlers mounted along the cornice, circling the entire room.

The bunks were all empty except for the far corner, closest to the fire, where a mattress and sleeping bag were rolled out, a duffle bag and tangle of clothes and cold gear spread out on the next bunk. An orange hunting coat with a license on the back and a white down jacket hung on hooks.

She went over and busied herself with the fire, arranging a few logs on the coals, adjusting the pile with an iron poker and tossing the rest of the apple on top. He looked for a place to set the beer down, which wasn't easy because the tabletop was completely littered with things: topographic maps, coffee mugs and empty beer cans, some weird-looking boxy rifle he'd never seen before, as well as a lever-action deer rifle with open sights, boxes of ammo shells—30-30 Winchester and .22—a stack of paper targets and thumbtacks, binoculars, sunglasses, and gloves.

At the far end of the table, a strange contraption was set up—a set of red-iron clamps holding down an inward-bowed arc of wood. Alongside were various tin cans with handwritten labels written in sharpie marker: "30-32° Soft," "19-30° Fresh," "5-25° Old," "Slushy," "Icy", and a big block of cork. Against the opposite wall, sets of long and thin skis were propped up in a row.

"Nice place," he said, and she shot him a look to see if he was being a wise-ass.

The logs in the fireplace were catching, ribbons of flame curling out from underneath. She collapsed in a heap into one of the chairs and let out a deep breath, as if all that wood chopping finally caught up with her.

"Bring me a beer," she said, and gestured toward the other seat. They cracked the cans open with a satisfying hiss and raised a toast. The beer was so clear and cold he could barely taste it as he swallowed.

"All right," she said with a sigh. "Fire away. I can see you've got questions."

He cleared his throat, realizing he had barely said a word this whole time. "What are you doing out here all by yourself."

"I'm not alone," she said. "I've got my dogs." Another flash of smile. "But seriously, this is my little hide-out. I come up here to train," she glanced over at the skis. "Biathlon."

And seeing that was not registering with him, she added, "You know, the one where you go cross country skiing and then you stop and shoot at targets."

"Oh, yeah. Now I know what you mean. I've seen the Winter Olympics on TV. But I didn't know anybody, you know, actually does that. I mean, nobody from here."

"Well, now you do. And it turns out I'm pretty good at it." She gave a little mock-humble bow, then continued. "I already know your next one. So my real name is Kathi, which I've always hated. And growing up I went by Kate, which isn't much better."

She took a deep drink, as if to brace herself, then launched into a story. "A few years ago, I was out living in Long Beach, California, in the off-season, with my ex. He was a downhill skier. You know, those guys that bomb down the mountain at 100 miles per hour? Well I met him during the tour over in Europe. He had such great legs …"

Stef had barely been out on a date, except maybe a school dance, and here she was talking to him about her ex. He tried to nod along as if he totally understood, but he was on thin ice.

"Anyway I realize now that wasn't the best reason to fall for a guy. I thought, *he's a skier, he must love the mountains, the winter, maybe liked hunting ...*" she shook her head. "Turns out he hated the cold. He was good at skiing because his rich parents spent winters in Vail, Aspen. He would much rather be surfing."

"So in the off season I went back with him to his beach place, which was jam packed with all these surfer dudes around the clock. And to keep training I got these roller-blade skis, and practiced on the trails along the beach." With the beer in hand, she gestured in a wavy motion from side to side. "His buddies thought it was hilarious and started calling me Skate. And so the start of the next season, he was doing some press—the guy *is* pretty famous—and they asked him about his girlfriend, and he called me 'Skate' and bam, it stuck." She took another sip and curled a smile. "Actually the one good thing to come out of the relationship."

Now that the fire was crackling, she leaned forward and tossed a couple more logs on. Heat was radiating out, with a heady smell of cherry wood and burnt apple. It quickly became hot sitting this close. She unzipped her hoodie and shrugged it off, revealing she was only wearing a white tank top underneath, her bare arms tattooed from wrist to shoulder, traced with runic letters and celtic knots, and at her shoulder a giant eagle clutching what looked like a swooning damsel-in-distress in its talons, ringed by red flame. A necklace with a turquoise pendant rested just below her collarbone.

He tried with everything in his power not to stare.

"So I needed to get away from living at the beach and remembered this place. Dad, he used to run the biggest hunting parties out of here. They'd have a dozen, sometimes more, stacked up to the rafters. Would drink, play cards all night long, then before dawn head out into the woods. I'm sure most fell asleep at their stands! But they bagged some big bucks." She nodded up at the antlers circling the room.

"I can't believe he let me come out here as a girl and hunt with that crew. It was pretty crude. They were all good ol' boys, but over-protective of me for sure, like I was everyone's daughter. Tried not to cuss around me—and failed. I learned to cross country ski out here—it's perfect—lots of lake-effect snow, lots of old logging trails, good elevation.

"Dad called this place 'Thunderbird'—the camp had been in our family forever—before this all was made state game land, but he's the one that carved the name above the door. He loved that brand of car, it's the only kind he ever drove."

She paused, took another gulp. "Then one night he wrecked it. Out late with the crew, probably drinking too much, someone coming other way with high beams on, blinded him for a moment, he swerved and went off the road. He was a giant of man, got pinned behind the steering wheel. Car burst into flames and they couldn't get him out."

She gave him a probing look. Stef didn't know what to say and so they sat there in silence listening to the wood pop and hiss. But she did not stay in reverie for long, just inhaled and resumed her story.

"I never knew my mom. Story goes, Dad went on one of his famous Canada trips into the backcountry, was gone for a full year, and when he returned, it was with me." She gave a little *ta-da* motion with her hands. "No questions asked."

"So after that I moved in with my grandpa. He's the one that got me into biathlon, figured I could ski, knew I could shoot. That's the tricky thing, there are really good skiers out there, tons of 'em. But it all comes down to shooting, coming out of the range with no misses. Being able to drop your pulse rate, steady your breathing. And hit the target. Turns out I'm a helluva shot. Thanks, Dad." She raised her beer can.

"Now Pops was never much for schooling," she continued. "He fancied the idea of me bringing home gold medals instead. He entered me in the first Nationals for women back in '80, and I was decent enough that he parlayed that into a spot on the new European Cup circuit. Shipped me overseas, pretty much on my own. I was seventeen. Learned quite a bit. Won a lot."

"So you are up here … training … for biathlon," Stef repeated slowly.

"And hunting. I'm here for that too. Mainly that."

"For how long?"

"Depends. On the snow, how I'm feeling. At this stage of my career, I'm pre-qualified for the World Championship. So maybe head back onto the circuit after Christmas. I'm in no rush."

She shook her can, tried to tilt out the last drop. Empty. She got up and stretched, now uncomfortably close to him, her belly button peeking out from beneath her shirt as she flexed her arms above her head. She walked over to the pantry shelves, rummaged around, and came back with two shot glasses and a bottle of bourbon. She poured each glass full to the rim, and delicately handed one to him.

"To sip," she said, sitting back down. "Cheers."

The fire was now in full blaze and it felt like he was swallowing some of it. He tried not to cough. She was looking straight at him with that even stare, light flickering in her pale blue eyes. "Now it's your turn. What's your story?"

He was quiet for a minute, his brow furrowed. "I guess I don't really have one."

"Well, that can be fixed," she said with that sharp smile of hers.

"Humor me," she continued. "Why are you way out here getting firewood? And how did you get past the gate?"

"It's my old man. He must have done some work for the Thiassens and they left him some wood, maybe as a favor. He knew right where the key was. Plus, he's always looking for opportunities to build character for me, so this was perfect for him. Actually, if you hadn't showed up, I don't know what I would've done."

"Had less firewood."

"Ha! So true." He shook his head. "We're opening up our camp tomorrow morning. My old man, me, my kid brother, my uncle who's arriving tomorrow, and a buddy of his, just the five us. Not crazy like some of the other hunting camps."

She watched him closely, sipping at her whiskey. "Are you looking forward to it, deer season?"

He stammered a little, not sure how to answer. "I mean, yeah. Of course I am."

"Do you know why?"

He felt flushed, from the bourbon and the roaring fire and the way she was looking at him. "I don't know. My family's always gone hunting. Like, it's just what you do. Never gave it much thought. Plus we have off school for the first and second days." The moment he said it, he regretted it, realizing how young it made him sound.

He tried to change the subject. "Must be pretty good hunting out here."

"Yeah, this is as close to a hunter's paradise as you'll find anywhere. Most days I don't see another person in the woods. Though Frost Hall does ferry up some hunters here on ATVs from time to time," she frowned.

She pointed directly above him to the wall, where a monster ten-point rack was mounted. "Last year," she said. From his close vantage, he could see the brainpan still stained pink, dandruff in the fur from the bone saw. "I was hunting further up the grade, at the head-end of Naval Hollow, near the old Fire Tower. In some pretty thick stuff, slashings. There were signs everywhere, buck rubs. Right at dusk, at last light, just when I was about to pack it in, he came down the trail. I just saw his silhouette. Had to spend the night out there."

"Spend the night?"

She shrugged as if it were no big deal. "Sometimes when I'm skiing and a storm comes up, gotta just hunker down and ride it out. I've got a nice little lightweight tent that's perfect."

"You know when I heard you say Naval Hollow, I just realized where we hunt isn't actually that far from here, I think. We mainly hunt in and around South Fork."

"That spring out back?" she said. "That flows into one of the hollows that becomes South Fork valley."

"Don't you think its strange how all the creeks are named out here? South Fork is north of here … North Fork is to the east … East Branch is to the west. Straight Creek is all crooked … and Crooked Creek runs straight!

"It's easy to get mixed up," she agreed. "We always called those hollows at the end of South Fork 'The Fortress'. Once deer got up in that country, it was next to impossible to get them out."

"Yeah, we call it that too! Its sort of shaped like a turkey-foot print, with three deep hollows at the end." He held out three fingers and she nodded. "Though to be honest, I've never been as far in as

The Fortress, only seen it on a map. We come into South Fork from below, way down at the bottom end," pointing into the crook of his elbow. "By boat. I know, I know, it's nuts. One of these years it's going to end in a rescue operation," he laughed.

"I haven't hunted much down there," she said. "You have any luck?"

"Me? Well. No, I haven't got my buck yet." He sat up, becoming animated. "Actually turns out it's my kid brother who's the lucky one. He just started hunting and got his buck each of the last two years. Two for two. Each at like, seven in the morning of the first day. Gets to his stand, waits about ten minutes, and bang!" He shook his head. "The golden child."

"You sound jealous."

He glared over at her at that remark, but she stared right back, locking eyes with him. He broke her gaze and looked over at the fire.

"I guess, maybe …" he said, trailing off.

"Hey, don't be sore," she said softly. "Do you want to have another round?"

He looked out the window. While they were talking it had turned pitch black outside. Then back at her, the firelight dancing in her jet-black hair...

Suddenly he snapped back to his senses, as if coming out of a trance. "I–I gotta get back," he announced, more to himself than to her. "My old man will be wondering where I got to."

He stood up stiffly, and she did too. Now she was very close to him, and he realized how tall she was, looking him eye to eye. He smelled wood smoke and apples, whiskey and sweat.

"You sure?" she asked.

He swallowed and nodded.

Outside it was purplish black, the dome of the sky clear and cold, the brightest stars beginning to prick through, a faint blue glow to the southwest in the wake of the sunset, a narrow horned moon tilting just above the horizon. The truck and the Jeep were nothing more than blocky impressions in the dark. When he opened the passenger door, the cab light provided some illumination.

She was standing in the doorway watching him, outlined in flickering orange firelight.

"Thanks again for all the help," he said. Then, with a crack in his voice, "Will I see you again?"

"Now you know where to find me," she replied. "Good luck on Monday."

"You too."

The engine rumbled to life. Backing out and turning around, as the headlights swung around in an arc, piercing through the forest in a jumble of sticks and shadows. He realized he had no idea how to retrace the way back to the grade, not in the dark.

Then he spied little glints on the trees—cat's-eye reflective tacks—marking the way forward like airport runway lights. As he crested the rise, he stole a glance in the rearview and saw her shape still standing in the door.

Pulling back onto the main grade road felt like the on-ramp to a four-lane highway. He picked up some speed and saw a flash out of the corner of his eye. The wolf dogs were chasing alongside the truck, one on each side, every few strides bounding up so he could see their faces just a foot away in the sideview mirrors, tongues lolling out, hungry eyes.

After a few hundred yards, they lost interest and pulled back. He stopped a ways further, looked back, and saw their shadows milling about in the red of the taillights. Then, in a blink, they vanished into the night.

✦

He parked the truck in the driveway turnaround out by the old barn, under the giant silver maple tree, by the basketball hoop. He could see his mom moving around in the kitchen. She had been up at dawn to go grocery shopping, working off the same handwritten list they'd saved and reused year after year. All day long she was cooking for camp, had started before he drove out to the grade in the morning and still at it.

From the little square window by the back stairs, he could see lights were on in the basement. His old man and kid brother would be down there, going through the equipment checklist, another hand-written list that didn't change from year to year. Everything in the same boxes where they had left them last year, but they still had to methodically go through them once again.

He quietly entered through the mud-room door, making sure the screen door didn't slam, sat on the bench, and took off his boots.

"Hey Mom, I'm back!" he finally called out.

"Took you longer than we thought," she called back.

He breathed in a jumbled smell of cooking—turkey noodle soup, vegetable soup with beef cubes, spaghetti sauce, pumpkin pies—then suddenly became aware of himself, the smell of smoke in his clothes and whiskey on his breath.

"Mom, I'm really sweaty. That was a lot of wood. I think I'm just going to run up and take a shower."

He quickly darted up the back stairs two at a time. "We already ate dinner, but there's a plate out here for you," she said, turning away from the stovetop to face him, but he was already upstairs.

"Stef?" his old man yelled up from the basement. "Is Stef back? Stef! How did it go?"

"Great! The truck is full of firewood!" he yelled back down the stairs. "Now I'm going to take a shower."

Another yell from the basement. "Marie! Tell Stef that JR and me are down in the basement getting the gear ready!"

"I'm going to take a shower!!" Stef shouted back, and slammed the door of the bathroom shut.

He ran the water until it was hot, turned on the shower, and undressed, jamming his clothes to the bottom of the laundry basket. He stared at his body in the mirror. Skinny, some wiry muscles, a mop of hair that could use a haircut if he was being honest. Barely a hint of stubble even though he hadn't shaved since before Thanksgiving. Nothing that stood out.

The mirror started to fog over.

After the shower, he toweled off, brushed his teeth just to be safe, and scampered down the hall to his room. It was cold and drafty upstairs in this old house. This used to be his grandparents home then, after they passed, his family moved here from just up the street.

He put on sweatpants and a hoodie, warm socks, and was about to head back downstairs to eat, but first went over to his writing desk and switched on the little lamp. There was a big USGS quad map tacked up to the wall there and, spread out across the desk, graph paper, colored pencils, and marker pens. One of his hobbies was making maps, and he was working on one of the area where they hunted.

He spent a few moments standing there, staring at the topographic map, trying to piece together where he was today, and how it connected with the rest. Then he noticed his mom had laid an envelope on his desk chair. It was addressed to him, but was already opened.

He took out the contents. It was cream linen paper, with the college logo centered in the letterhead. *"Dear Mr. Stefan Yeager, We are pleased to inform you ..."*

The letter also contained a glossy brochure with a fold-out cover, showing the college campus with the Philadelphia skyline in the background. A girl in a summer dress and a guy in a polo shirt walked side by side down a tree-lined brick walkway, books in arms, laughing about something.

He put the letter and the brochure back in the envelope and sat down on the chair, staring at the maps on his desk.

SATURDAY

Nestled deeply under the covers, he was woken by the shock of an ice-cold hand gripping his shoulder and shaking him.

"Rise and shine!"

His old man yanked open the curtains to reveal a gray, smudgy dawn. Stef groaned and rolled over, pulling the blankets up over his head. His old man sat down in the desk chair, next to the radiator, looking out the window at the new day, and started talking like he always did.

"That's a nice piece of work you did yesterday. I didn't think you had it in you. Like the work of two men."

Stef remained quiet and motionless underneath the blankets, hoping his old man would get distracted, move on, and let him grab a few more minutes of sleep. *Why didn't his kid brother ever get this early morning treatment?*

"I made a phone call this morning," his old man announced.

Who made phone calls at 7 a.m.?

"Let them know you'd be coming along with us tonight."

That got Stef's attention. Each year on the Saturday before the first day of buck season, his old man, the General, and the General's best friend—Mac—were invited to a big hunting feast down at Frost Hall. There had never been any suggestion that Stef—or anyone younger than the hills, for that matter—ever attended. Typically, he had spent Saturday night home in town, and then on Sunday his mom drove Stef and his kid brother—once JR had started hunting—down to their family's camp. The whole feast was shrouded in mystery.

"This morning we'll take the supplies down to Hilo. Should be back by the time the General arrives." The chair creaked as his old man got up, boots on the hardwood floor as walked toward the door. Stef pressed his eyes shut tight, clinging to the last threads of sleep.

The footsteps stopped by the bed. "Your mother told me about the letter," he said quietly. In his sleep, Stef had totally forgotten about that. His old man reached in under the blankets and rubbed his knuckles hard into the muscles of Stef's upper back. "I'm proud of you, son."

Stef mumbled something inaudible in reply, his face mushed in the pillow.

"Now, up and at 'em. Roll 'em out, cowboy!"

After breakfast, they loaded up the Oldsmobile with gear and supplies. In the back seat, they built up a cushion of sleeping bags around the encased rifles so that nothing could fall on top of them and jostle the scopes. On the floor of the passenger side of the truck, his mom carefully arranged the crocks of soup and sauce and taped down the lids so they wouldn't spill. The cans of gasoline went in the back of the truck, wedged among the firewood.

His old man and kid brother went together in the Olds and Stef followed behind in the truck. There was a frost overnight and as they drove out of town the fields were steel gray and glistening in the morning sun. They ascended Hel's Hill, the truck making a rumbling and wheezing sound, shuddering as if about to go into cardiac arrest. The crest looked out across the chasm to the top of Shawmut Grade, still in shadow, maybe three miles as the crow flies but feeling like another country away with the deep valley in between.

The road squiggled like a piece of spaghetti, woods and sharp drop offs on either side, here and there passing a usually empty double-wide trailer or hunting camp, now with pickup trucks and ATVs jammed in alongside, some overflowing and parked on the berm of the road. The camps had names like "Wolfe's Den," "Pancake Palace," "Camp Bat," and his personal favorite "The R&G Club" which maybe for the wives stood for Rod & Gun, but everyone knew really meant Ruttin' and Guttin'. Any camp where people stood outside, his old man slowed down the station wagon and made sure to wave.

At the base of Hel's Hill, they took the hairpin turn, crossed the bridge over Crooked Creek, rounded the bend at Middle Fork where the game commission had their ranger station, then another bridge across the East Branch, and up the hill to the dam.

The long and deep V-shaped valley of the East Branch was carved out over millennia, but after the city of Pittsburgh had historic flooding on St. Patrick's Day, 1936—the result of record snows that winter, a rapid thaw, and torrential rains—that all changed. The Army Corps of Engineers were given the authority to construct a series of flood-control dams along the Allegheny watershed, and this lonely valley far at the upper reach was the just right specifications.

So the Corps condemned the entire valley upstream from Middle Fork, which included a little half-empty logging town, and built a giant earth-and-concrete dam across the narrows, flooding the entire valley for eight miles, entombing the town under a hundred feet of water.

The remaining land that wasn't underwater was made into a state park, except for one valley—now a cove on the lake—where by coincidence the land had been snatched up by Thiassen in a timely transaction, just before construction was announced. The company had connections in Harrisburg, and everyone looked the other way. Thiassen in turn parceled lakefront lots out to long-time company men and loyal business associates—men like Stef's grandpa, who was the banker in town and handled Thiassen's accounts—who each in turn built their own little lakeside getaway, about twenty camps in all.

In the summer the dam was full, the encircling hilltops deep green and lush, the camps and docks filled with families, boats making lazy circles, pulling water-skiers in tow. But in the winter the Corps emptied half the lake in preparation for the spring thaw, exposing raw hillsides, the topsoil and tree-stumps long since washed away, just barren rocks left behind.

The way in was a poorly maintained dirt road that started near the main breastwork and traced the shoreline around the first inlet where Swamp Creek flowed into the lake. His old man made sure to stop as they passed by the Sauer camp, which had a dozen trucks crammed in the turnabout and as nearly as many kegs stacked outside. An American flag was raised on the flagpole.

A bunch of guys were milling about on the front porch with plastic beer cups, some smoking, others with wads of chew, including Fred Sauer, who was the foreman down at Thiassen Powdered Metal, as well as his twin sons Cole and Chase, who were a few years older than Stef. Both of them were top wrestlers, both made it to the state tourney, where one of them famously dropped a weight class so they wouldn't have to face each other—though Stef couldn't remember which one— and then both were recruited to Penn State's nationally ranked wrestling team.

His old man called out, "Hey Fred! I brought you a staple gun. Works a lot better than string for fixin' antlers on a doe!" The men all guffawed even though Stef thought it was pretty lame, like most of the old man's jokes.

"Bring it by tomorrow!" Fred Sauer called back. "You can give us a seminar, Jack, you being an expert and all. Remember that buck you shot where the horns fell off?" More laughter.

"Expensive deer," his old man replied.

Then Fred sobered up and asked "The General?" All the men around got quiet.

"Arriving this afternoon," his old man said.

Fred gave a short nod, satisfied. And with a wave, they drove on. The twins stared at Stef as he drove past in the truck, one of them spitting, though Stef couldn't tell which.

A few hundred yards further they reached the turnoff for their camp, marked by a little sign that read 'HILO,' which stood for 'high from the water, low from the road.' They eased the vehicles down the steep driveway and parked on the bricked patio in front of the camp, a one-story cinderblock structure painted brick red, with white-trimmed picture windows in the front and a screened-in sunporch attached on the left side.

His kid brother hopped out and went over to the tiny statue of St. Anthony, standing in a little wooden shrine nailed to the big maple beside the camp. He lifted it up and retrieved the front door key from beneath the saint's feet. Inside, the camp was as cold as a refrigerator.

They each had a pretty clear idea of what tasks needed to be done and who was doing what, so they just went right into it without really talking. They got the ancient electric heaters out of the shed and plugged them into equally ancient sockets, and the coils began to glow orange, the fans rattled and coughed, and a smell like burnt hair came out. Then his old man turned on the water, which was always chancy. Would any left-behind liquid have frozen and burst the pipes? But it had been a mild fall so far and they were in luck, no jets of water spraying anywhere.

They set up a relay to stack the firewood, his kid brother up in the truck, Stef acting as the back and forth, his old man building up a crib at either end of the pile and then filling in the space between, shaking his head, amazed at the amount of split wood.

They put the crocks of soups, sauce, and pies—along with the rifles—out on the sunporch, stacked the dry goods in the cabinets, filled the kitchen fridge from the coolers, then stored the beer in the empty coolers out on the sunporch so it wouldn't freeze. His kid brother rolled out the sleeping bags and placed fresh pillowcases on. They checked for any mice in the traps, found three, and tossed them over the front bank.

They carried the five-gallon tanks of gas down stone stairs leading to the shoreline. The dock was still in the water, but just barely, with most of the ramp now onshore because of the falling water level. They loosened the guide ropes, heaved the ramp down to the water-line, and then re-tied them, lifted up a corner of the boat cover to get access to the gas cap, and poured in the fuel, some of it inevitably sloshing into the lake and causing a rainbow slick to spread out. Stef looked up and around at the encircling bowl of bare-rock hillsides, and the caked mudflats at the end of the cove where Swamp Creek ran in. Everything was brown-gray and lifeless, like they were on the surface of another planet.

Back at the camp, a faint trace of warmth emerged from the wheezing heaters. They took a moment to wolf down ham-and-cheese hoagies from the deli in town. In the fireplace, they prepared a fire, using dead branch tips from the pine tree out front as kindling, crum-pling up some old newspaper, building a crib of logs around it, so one match strike would light it when they returned later that night.

By the time they made it back to town, a wood-paneled station wagon with Virginia plates and a bumper sticker with four stars was parked in the driveway. Inside, the General and Mac were in the kitchen talking to his mom.

You wouldn't know the General was an Army general by looking at him. He had on a red shirt, a red down vest, brown hunting pants, and a blaze-orange hunting cap. He really looked like just an older, more dignified-looking version of Stef's old man. Maybe it was the way he checked his watch, putting two fingers on the cuff of his shirt and a brisk slide-back to reveal the watch face—not the watch itself, either, which was an ordinary watch and band, nothing fancy—but how often he checked it, nearly every other minute, like clockwork.

Mac looked even less like a military guy, though he also was a general—having two stars to the General's four—also went to West Point, also served in Korea and in Vietnam as did the General. He was an engineer, mild-mannered, quiet, always deferential toward his good friend the General. Mac was wearing a hunter green wool shirt and matching pants, and had a smile on his face and a twinkle in his eye. It was clear that coming up here for hunting season and the chance to see all of the characters in town was a highlight for him.

The adults all exchanged pleasantries, asking about family members, who was where and doing what. From the television in the other room came the play-by-play of a college football game and Stef's attention wandered as he tried to make out the teams and the score.

Then, as if some critical minute on the watch dial had been crossed, the General inhaled sharply and said, "All right."

The chit chat abruptly ended and the conversation shifted. "Licenses, Mass, then Frost Hall," his old man said, ticking off items on a mental checklist. "We took the supplies to Hilo this morning."

The General nodded.

He took a step forward to give Stef's mom a kiss on the cheek, Mac followed suit, and then in a blink they were back outside getting into vehicles.

Hammerschmidt's was located in the center of town, just down the street from his old man's law office, on the other side of the railroad tracks, catty-corner from the savings and loan where Stef's grandpa had worked. They parked in the nearby municipal lot and walked down the block to the store, the General carrying his rifle case in one hand. A few people in front of the five and dime stopped and stared.

While the General and Mac went up to the counter to apply for licenses, his old man launched into a yarn with Jeff Hammerschmidt about the buck JR tagged last year. His kid brother played right along with an aw-shucks expression.

Stef wandered around the store, looking up at the grand twenty-foot high tin-plated ceiling and the elaborate hanging light fixtures. The high walls were crammed with all kinds of taxidermy: ducks, pheasants, ruffed grouse, even a tiny woodcock—posed mid-flight—a bobcat, a turkey, an owl, raccoons, a beaver, a weasel-like fisher—perched on little rock outcroppings or tree branches—a whole school of monster trout, walleye, muskies, and bass, plus scores of mounted trophy bucks, and an elk, as well as some that weren't from around here like a moose head and a bighorn ram.

The shop floor had tables with a variety of shirts, pants, socks, gloves, and long johns. Along the right wall were racks of hunting coats and overalls, hip waders and fishing vests. On the opposite wall, rifles and shotguns were displayed behind a long glass counter filled with knives, scopes, and boxes of ammo. The back of the store had the fly rods and special display cases for flies they tied here themselves, with a little work table and bins of tying materials for when they gave classes.

Stef got lost for a few minutes looking at all the various flies, trying to figure out which were wet and which dry, what sorts of hatches each matched, some of the more complicated ties, like the grasshopper—one of his personal favorites. For a moment he could picture summer in his mind, a distant memory of lush green hills, a slowly moving stream at sunset, a haze of bugs hatching and trout jumping, hot and humid.

After they got the licenses squared away and signed them, the General unzipped the case and took out the rifle. It was an exotic gun nobody had seen before, a custom-built rifle that the General received as a gift from the president of Argentina, with a woodgrain stain that was almost greenish in hue, an enormous scope, an elaborate embossed leather strap. It looked more like a sniper rifle than something to hunt deer.

A discussion ensued about whether the 7.62 NATO and .308 Win shells were interchangeable. Jeff Hammerschmidt and several other employees came over, and pretty quickly two schools of thought emerged: one, they were perfectly interchangeable, and the other, that you can use 7.62 NATO in a .308 but not vice versa. After some back and forth, it was decided the General shouldn't bother with the fancy gun at all, but use Stef's grandpa's tried-and-true 30-06 instead. Nods of agreement came from all around.

The General pulled out a roll of bills and paid for both out-of-state licenses with a crisp fifty-dollar bill. Lots of well wishes and good lucks and questions about the health of Hammerschmidt family members followed, as well as an invitation to come up to their annual fly-fishing outing up on the Prouty over Memorial Day weekend, which the General said he would take under consideration.

As they came out of the store, the sun was already beginning to set. They parked back at the house and walked down the street to Our Lady of the Woods, its gothic steeple like a black finger against the crimson and purple clouds, the stained glass windows lit from within in a rainbow of color. The bells chimed as they mounted the front stairs, dipped a finger in the holy water, and made signs of the cross. The ushers handed out weekly bulletins and one of them, wearing a VFW pin on the lapel of his sport coat, straightened up and saluted. The General snapped a crisp return salute.

The church was packed with people—far more than regularly attended—but his mom had saved a row near the front for them, and looking back, she saw them enter and waved. As they walked up the aisle, his old man stopped at nearly every pew, patted people on the shoulder, made eye contact, and gave quick waves. The General doled out a few nods and handshakes as well. Only the first groaning notes of the organ rolling into the introductory hymn brought the meet and greet to a close. They slid into the pew, and even then his old man made a point to turn around and say hello to the folks in the row behind.

The church was built in the Gothic style, a high vaulted ceiling criss-crossed with ribs, corinthian columns, heavy iron chandeliers hanging from chains, tall arched stained glass along the side walls and in a semi-circle behind the altar, and a choir balcony in the rear where the pipe organ was located. The walls on the sides and columns were a cream color, the column capitals painted gold and the ceiling a deep Prussian blue with gold constellations traced out. Behind the altar, the walls were painted blood red and a crucifix hung suspended on wires, floating in the air above the golden tabernacle. An elaborate wooden screen—made of black cherry wood carved with celtic knots and twisted braids, a three-leaf-clover motif atop each panel and mesh see-through screens—divided the space so seniors with walkers and wheelchairs could enter from the side and be able to see the mass up close without disturbing everyone.

To the left of the altar a statue of the Virgin Mary leaned forward as if into a gale-force wind, wrapped in a blue robe, one arm up as a shield and the other cradling the infant Jesus, who was tranquil, playing happily with a golden orb. At the rail that divided the altar from the nave, banks of votive candles glowed softly in blue and white.

A bell jingled and the priest and altar boys entered from a door on the side. Father Blaise was wearing a black biretta cap with a purple pom-pom on top, purple vestments trimmed in gold, bifocals, and a humorless expression as firm as ironwood. As the last warbling notes of the organ faded, he immediately launched into the service, looking upward into the vaulted ceiling as he almost sang the liturgy in a deep baritone voice, oblivious to the packed church.

Stef had served mass for all of the priests at Our Lady of the Woods, and even though Father Blaise was old school and might tug your robes or even cuff you right out in the open if you were doing something wrong, he was all business and said the mass at a brisk pace, not like some of the other priests who always found the longest, most arcane rites, like the one that listed all the saints down to Cyril and Methodius—whoever they were—or brought out the censer and waved it clanking until the whole church was in a fog of incense. No, Father Blaise had little patience and brooked no interruptions. If some hapless parent brought a crying baby, Father Blaise would glare at them—continuing to say mass, not breaking stride, maintaining his stare—until the baby stopped or the parent scurried the child out the back in shame.

When the time came for his sermon, he gripped the sides of the lectern. "I see a lot of new faces here tonight," he intoned, his voice booming. "Family and friends who moved away, returning home for deer season. Welcome. We wish all safety and luck on Monday. And on this occasion, with so many of you present, there is an important message I would like to share with you."

He pulled a square of paper from beneath his robes, unfolded it loudly in front of the microphone, adjusted his bifocals, cleared his throat, and let his eyes rove across the congregation. "We need $10,000 to fix the roof. Please open your wallets and be generous."

He folded up the paper and tucked it back beneath his robes. "And don't forget our annual Pre-Buck Season Potato Pancake Dinner at the school cafeteria, immediately after tonight's service. There will be a 50-50 raffle."

An advent wreath made of ground pine had been set up by the lectern, a pail of holy water and a wand at its base. Father Blaise said a blessing over the wreath, then cajoled the altar boys out of their stupor and, after several attempts, they got one of the candles lit, then together they marched up and down the aisles, Father Blaise waving the wand with vigor, flinging a rain of holy water left and right, as if he were dispelling demons, the altar boys' robes nearly drenched by the end of the procession.

Then the collection plate made its rounds. His mom already had an envelope prepared, and out of the corner of his eye Stef saw the General and Mac each put in hundred-dollar bills.

At the Eucharist, everyone knelt and Father Blaise held the communion wafer above his head and sang, "Take this all of you and eat it, for this is my body which will be given up for you." An altar boy jingled the little set of bells. Then Father Blaise raised a golden cup, "Take this all of you and drink from it, for this is the chalice of my blood." Another round of ringing.

At the end of mass the organist boomed out an advent hymn and everyone sang along. Father Blaise made his way to the main entrance to greet the parishioners as they shuffled their way out. When the General reached him, a sort of transformation occurred and a warm smile cracked the priest's stern visage. He became almost bashful. The General inquired about the health of his sister, who had been a high-school classmate of the General's.

His old man asked about Sister Mary Magdalene and if she were going out this year. "Wouldn't miss it for the world," Father Blaise said smiling. The nun's picture had been on the front page of the newspaper last year, posing with her rifle and the enormous ten-point buck she bagged.

Father Blaise invited them to the potato pancake dinner, but his old man mentioned they were headed down to camp tonight, and the priest understood. Stef had been trying to hang back but Father

Blaise caught his eye. Stef braced to be called out for some mistake, like not paying attention during the service, but the priest solemnly made a quick sign of the cross. "May Our Lady watch over you."

It was pitch dark outside as they walked back up the street to the house. There was another round of goodbyes, his kid brother on one side with his mom, a hang-dog look on his face, and Stef standing on the other side with the men. Then they all piled into the vehicles for the drive down to Frost Hall.

⁓�𝔬𝔤⁓

Travelling out of town east on West Creek Road, just past the powdered metal plant and the turnoff for the Shawmut Grade, the road plummeted down the face of the continental divide. Stef rode in the truck with his old man, the General and Mac followed in the station wagon. The AM radio was tuned to the big Notre Dame–USC football game, but the reception was pure static. That didn't faze his old man, he knew what was happening based on the modulation of noise and the occasional snippet of play-by-play that came across.

"Southern Cal turned it over," he proclaimed after one squelching burst. A few minutes later, a sustained high-pitched hiss on the radio and he stated matter-of-factly, "Irish touchdown."

At the bottom of the mountain, the road crossed the steel-girder bridge over West Creek. They turned left onto an unmarked gravel road and soon came to a set of giant twenty-foot-high wrought-iron gates, embossed with the circle, arrow, and stars of the Thiassen logo, and at the top of the arch, a cut-out image of two bucks sparring with their antlers.

His old man pulled the truck alongside a metal post topped with an intercom, cranked down the window, leaned out, and pressed the red button. There was a garble of noise that was no problem for him to decipher. "It's Jack Yeager," he replied.

An electric motor whirred to life and the iron gates clanked, squealed, and swung inward. The gravel road cut through a dense thicket of old-growth hemlock, like passing through a tunnel. Then the trees parted and provided a vista across North Fork creek to Frost Hall.

The lodge was situated in the middle of the deepest part of the valley, with both hillsides rising almost vertically like canyon walls overhead and a narrow ribbon of starry sky far above. Spotlights shined on the exterior from every angle, making Frost Hall gleam like a jewel against black velvet.

The building was designed to look like a Viking longhouse, with a high pitched roof and carved antlers jutting upward at the apex of the gables at each end. Parked out front in the circular driveway were a number of black Suburbans and super-duty pickup trucks emblazoned with the Thiassen logo, as well as a few luxury cars. In the center of the turnabout, an oversized American flag hung atop a flagpole, lit from below by lights.

The left wing of the longhouse was encased on three sides in windows that looked out across a terrace, a sweeping lawn that led to an outdoor pavilion situated next to a fishing pond. Inside, a near-bonfire was roaring in the stone hearth, men in zip-fleeces and flannel shirts were seated on leather couches and armchairs, swilling glasses of whiskey and goblets of wine. The doors to the terrace were open and another fire had been built there in the fire-pit, more men standing around it, smoking cigars.

They drove across the stone bridge leading up toward Frost Hall, but instead of continuing to the front entrance they turned left onto a narrow path that was really just two bumpy tire tracks that curved away from the main lodge and plunged back into the dense hemlock. Stef turned his head around and saw the gleaming outline of Frost Hall grow smaller until it was just a glow of light through the trees, then they made a sharp turn into a narrow side draw and the night swallowed it up.

Stef looked over at his old man, his face lit by the faint light from the dashboard, eyes on the narrow path ahead, still listening to the steady drone coming from the radio. This deep in the ravine, reception was a lost cause. Nothing seemed out of the ordinary with him.

Another sharp turn around a boulder and suddenly a little cabin appeared in the center of a clearing. All of the lights were on inside and at least a dozen vehicles were outside. They found a place where they wouldn't get stuck and parked the truck, the General pulling his station wagon alongside.

"I thought we were going to Frost Hall," Stef said.

His old man shook his head as if that were a silly question. "Frost Hall's for tourists."

The night was clear, the Milky Way visible overhead. He felt the cold of the valley hit his nostrils along with the tang of wood smoke, heard the roar of an invisible brook cascading down from the cliff face somewhere in the darkness, and, from inside the camp, the noise of a party in full swing.

When they entered, there was a shout of greeting all around.

"Jack! General! Mac!"

Stef hung back, barely inside the door, as hearty hugs and handshakes were exchanged. The main room was divided by a central fireplace that was open on both sides. The near side was a sitting area with some couches, a coffee table, and a record player and speakers on top of an ancient TV set that was tuned to the football game and not getting much better reception than the car radio had. On the other side of the fireplace was a dining area with a long table, a kitchen and bar to the left, and a door that led back to the bunkroom. The walls were wood-paneled and hung with various animal pictures—hunting dogs, a grouse, a pheasant, a leaping buck—and above the fireplace was mounted a twelve-point buck's head, regally looking off into the distance. Easily twenty people were jammed into the tiny camp, and Stef recognized most of them.

Bunny, who was his old man's first cousin and sidekick in all kinds of shenanigans back in the day, was in full regale when they entered, telling the story of the time Jack and Bunny went fishing up in Canada, how each day when they came back to their camp a bear had gotten into their tents, so they drove to the nearest town, bought six cans of chili and hot sauce, mixed them up in a pan and left it out for the bear, who crept into their camp that night, wolfed down the chili and, with a loud "Woof," huffed down to the lake and jumped in, thrashing about with its mouth open. That bear didn't bother them again.

Oscar, a gruff old timer that retired from Thiassen Carbon—his old man had represented him on a black-lung claim, unsuccessfully, because when the judge asked how his health had been impaired, Oscar answered, "I used to be able to climb Hel's Hill behind my house without stopping. Now I have to stop once or twice to catch my breath." At the time of the claim, Oscar was in his seventies.

Doc, sporting a full white mustache, owned the gas station and repair shop in town where they always got their cars fixed, which was a regular occasion—his old man insisted on buying used cars and drove them until they died. Stef had plenty of memories stranded on the side of the road—usually passing the time by fishing in some nearby trout stream—until Doc arrived, honking, to give them a tow.

Others he knew vaguely: Bootsy and Tater and Burr and Pumpkin, and Dickie, who was an artist and famous fly-tier. And a bunch of men in their thirties who he gathered worked up at Frost Hall as hunting guides.

Finn was in the back of the room with a fiddle, playing some old Irish dirge. He wore a trucker's cap perched awkwardly on top of his head with a slight list. Finn was a well-known builder in town—he was the one that made the black cherry panel screens at Our Lady of the Woods. Being Irish—and without permission—he cut the three-leaf-clover motif on top of each panel, which angered the priests, but most folks in town approved.

Standing next to him listening, a glass of whiskey in hand, was none other than Karl Thiassen himself, the owner of Thiassen Industries. He stood head and shoulders above everyone else, easily six-foot-six, with hair nicely combed into a part off to the side, wearing a wool sweater, thick glasses, and a bemused look on his face.

Fred Sauer was standing nearby, and off in the corner Stef spotted the twins, Chase and Cole.

Then he saw Skate.

She was listening to the Sauer twins talking. They had sort of cut her off from the main party and backed her into the far corner, but her face had the same neutral expression he'd seen before, unconcerned. She stood nearly a head above the twins, who were short and wiry wrestler types. Her black hair was in pigtails, and she was wearing a white down jacket, unzipped so her turquoise necklace was visible, her hands tucked in the pockets of her jeans, the firelight playing on her cheekbones. She caught him staring and gave him a little wave, a curl of a smile.

Both the Sauer twins' heads snapped around in sync, and seeing him there, frowned.

Just then Bunny shouted from the kitchen. "Another case!"

His old man shouted back, "Stef can go fetch it!"

Doc approached him. "The beer's out in the spring house." Then, glancing over at his old man, added, "I think there's some cans of pop out there, too."

"Where's the spring house?" Stef asked.

"Follow the sound of the stream," Doc said with a wink, "and when your feet get wet, you've gone too far." There was no offer of a flashlight.

Outside, the exterior spots created a perfect cone of light around the camp, but beyond it was jet black. He was barely able to make out the outline of the tips of the hemlock trees against the starry sky. The sound from inside was muted when the front door closed, and he could hear the stream flowing. A frost had already formed on the grass, so his boots crunched as he walked. The stream grew louder as he entered the pines. He looked back and the tiny bubble of light around the camp seemed far away, the sound of the party drowned out by the sound of water.

His boots squished. He could sense more than see the bulk of a sheer cliff rising up to his left, the crash of water cascading down bare rock, the cold damp of mist in the air. By now, his eyes had adjusted enough to see the outline of a square cinderblock structure, a ghostly cube that seemed to hover in the dark. He felt his way over, certain at any moment he would plunge headlong into the stream he could hear all around him.

There was a door that swung outward and he had to tug hard on the handle, putting his whole back into it, to get it unwedged. Stepping inside was like entering a cave within a cave. The door swung shut behind him, the volume of the rushing water suddenly turned down. Zero visibility, the darkness making weird spots flicker in front of his eyes. The temperature felt one degree above freezing, but with the damp it felt much colder. He felt along the clammy cinderblock wall, terrified of what his hand might encounter.

A switch!

A little bare bulb cast the dimmest of light inside the spring-house, but to him it seemed like full high beams. It was a little square room, the walls spattered with mildew and water stains and cobwebs in all of the corners, some wires coming in from the outside, an electric pump, a pipe carrying water back to the camp.

On a metal table were stacked about a dozen cases of beer … and he spied a six-pack of pop cans on the floor underneath. He shook his head, but took the cans anyway, balanced them on top of a case of beer and hefted it—heavy as a block of ice. He fumbled around at the door, managed to hit the switch with his elbow, nudged the door open with his shoulder, and kicked it shut behind him with a backward flick of his foot.

When he returned, Skate was out standing on the porch by herself. She had on an orange tossle cap and had zipped up her jacket against the cold. She glanced at the picnic table under the eaves, and Stef put down the case of beer with a sigh of relief, the muscles in his shoulders burning by this point.

"So," she said.

"You're the last person I would have expected to run into here!" he blurted out.

"Am I?" she seemed genuinely puzzled by that.

Now up close, he noticed for the first time on her jacket, above her heart, a "USA Biathlon" patch with the name *Thiassen* embroidered underneath. He stared at her, speechless.

"You're Jack Yeager's boy," she said. "I should have noticed the resemblance. The same smile."

"You're ... part of the Thiassen family?"

"Pops in there is my grandpa. Chairman and CEO," she said. "I figured you would have put two and two together, especially when you talked to your dad ..."

She narrowed her eyes. "Oh. You didn't tell anyone." She let out a short bark of a laugh, her teeth flashing. "He must think you are Paul Bunyan with all that wood you chopped."

"I just—"

"Felt guilty? You Catholics. As my dad used to say, 'If you're gonna serve the time, you might as well commit the crime.'"

Stef felt his cheeks were on fire.

"Hey. I'm teasing," she said. "Your dad used to be a part of the crew up at Thunderbird. Bunny. Fred Sauer. I met them all when I was a girl…" She paused, then took a step closer. "Look. There's something you should know. Your dad was there … the night of the accident. Tried to pull him out of the car."

Stef stared at her.

"Let me guess. He never talked about it." Stef shook his head. "Well, that's not too much of a surprise. None of those guys do. That's men for you."

"I'm … I'm sorry."

"About what? That's all ancient lore now. *The Saga of Thunderbird Thiassen.* My dad was destined to go out in a fiery crash, that's how he lived his life, that's how his thread got snipped. Fate."

She let out a long exhale, a halo cloud of icy breath around her head, the reflected light from inside glinting in her eyes.

Then she smiled. "C'mon. Not so glum."

She reached into the case, found a bottle, twisted off the top, and took a long swig.

"Earlier," Stef said. "I saw you talking to the Sauer twins. Do you, um … know them well?"

"Ha! Those two. My curse is jocks. They mistake adrenaline for bravery, testosterone for toughness. Always one upping each other and everyone else. But in my experience, the first real test, they fold."

"I'm not a jock," Stef said quickly. "I basically suck at sports."

"Well, there's hope for you yet—"

Just then the front door to the camp swung open and Doc popped his head out. He saw the two of them standing there. "Oh, hi Kathi," he said. "Sorry to interrupt. Stef, we thought the coyotes had got you!"

Doc tapped a finger along the side of his nose. "They've been working up a powerful thirst in there."

"Okay, I'll be right in," Stef said. He hefted the case and lugged it toward the door, which Doc held open for him. He glanced back and she raised her beer.

"Skol!" she said.

And then Stef was back inside, thrust into the middle of the party. "Beer's here!" Doc called out. "Clear a path!" And to Stef: "Take 'er into the kitchen."

There were two fridges, one for food and the other for beer. He set the case on the bar counter and Doc started handing out bottles, flicking the lids off with a bottle opener shaped like a horse's ass. Once everyone who needed one got one, Doc did a quick relay with Stef to fill up the fridge. Then Doc said to Stef, "You must be thirsty." And handed him the six-pack of pop.

For the first time Stef got a close look at the cans. They weren't the usual aluminum, these were made of steel and so rusted it was impossible to make out the brand. They looked older than he was.

Doc, who was eyeing him closely, gave a small encouraging nod. Stef twisted a can free and suddenly became aware that the party noise had died down and eyes were on him.

Click-click-click, he couldn't get his fingernail underneath the pull-tab, it was fused to the lid of the can. "I can't get it open," Stef said.

Doc frowned, looked around at the rest of the men, and said, "Well, that settles it. You'll just have to drink beer!" he roared.

And the crowd laughed heartily, clearly in on the joke.

Doc handed him an open bottle, one of the big brown sixteen-ounce returnables from the brewery, cold and already dewy with condensation. The first sip was icy and crisp. His old man clapped him on the shoulder and everyone cheered.

Then Doc announced, "Dinner's ready!" and they made their way over to the long table. Finn sat at the head of the table and Karl Thiassen to his right. Everyone else sort of found their way to a place and Stef, coming in last from the kitchen, somehow ended up in a corner seat among the old men, just to the left of Finn, across from Karl Thiassen and the General, with Oscar at his side.

The table was simply set with a red-checked vinyl tablecloth, paper napkins, a mish-mash of silverware—except for the steak knives, which had handles made from antlers—and special plates, each with a different picture depicting an episode in history of the town: the loggers, the discovery of oil, coal mining, the church, the brewery, hunting and fishing, veterans of foreign wars. Dickie the artist had drawn the series, and Our Lady of the Woods auctioned off sets years ago, when Stef was a kid, to raise money to pay for the wooden screens behind the altar. His mom had bought a set, though they were only used for display, never to eat on.

Stef got the one about the town being founded during a blizzard, a lonely fire with people huddled around, in the middle of a dark hemlock forest with snow swirling about and wolves' eyes peering out from the shadows.

He looked around to see where Skate was and realized she hadn't come back in yet. At least he was far away from the Sauer twins who were glaring at him from the other end of the table. There didn't seem to be any empty seats left at the table. He wondered if maybe she could pull up a chair at this end, if Finn slid over? Or would that be too obvious if he suggested it.

Meanwhile Doc brought out platters of food. Roast venison tenderloin cut into thin medallions, venison sausages dripping with grease, bowls of venison chili with a dollop of sour cream, all from deer taken earlier that fall in archery season by the guides at Frost Hall. Sauerkraut and potato pancakes and applesauce with cinnamon. Thick slices of soft, Italian bread and butter.

Finn ceremoniously doffed his trucker's cap and nodded to the General, who stood and cleared his throat, and spoke with authority: "God bless this feast. Thank Him for bringing us all together here tonight. We pray for all those who have passed before us, may He be merciful. Please watch over and protect our armed forces. And lastly, dear Lord, please send a buck our way!"

"Amen!" everyone proclaimed. Then the platters were passed around, plates were loaded up, and everyone dug in.

Stef kept glancing at the front door, but there was no sign of her.

His old man, sitting between the General and Mac, across from Bunny, already had launched into one of his tales. "It was the winter of '76–77. The Big Freeze."

Murmurs all around the table.

"On Sunday it was fifty degrees. And a complete deluge opened up. We were down paying Oscar a visit and had to sight our guns in from his porch."

"By 7 a.m. on Monday, it was zero degrees. That whole week was below zero every day. We took the boat up to South Fork. I borrowed a .308 from Bunny. A four-point buck came by, but the gun only went off on the fifth try."

"The way it works, Jack, is—you have to pull the trigger," Bunny pantomimed, to laughs.

"I still got the deer," his old man said. "Then the lake froze over the second day. Mac here almost fell in."

Mac shook his head, smiling gamely, remembering.

"The General arrived on Wednesday. He hunted alone Thursday and Friday. The temperatures were twenty below each day. The two of us went out on Saturday morning on Hel's Hill and the General got a buck with one antler missing. I not only pointed out the deer, but told him when to shoot, gutted the deer, and dragged the deer out."

"Now Jack realizes how he got to be a General!" Bunny declared. More laughter around the table.

Stef became aware of Finn peering at him, one eye squinting and the other sharp and blue. His cheeks were a little flushed from the several glasses of whiskey he'd downed so far.

"When I was your age, I could piss over a telephone wire," Finn stated matter-of-factly, a little slur in his voice. He made an arc in the air with his hand to illustrate. Stef just nodded in response.

Finn next rolled up his sleeve. "Here, give me your hand. Feel this," He flexed his arm, which was as tough as oak. "Down the carpentry shop, I could lift a keg of nails." The tattoo on his forearm was of a topless island girl, the ink faded into blue and pink, and he made a point of squeezing his hand and making her breasts wiggle.

"United States Marine Corps," Finn said. "WW2."

"You can always tell a Marine," the General said, eavesdropping. "You just can't tell him much." Laughter.

Finn gave the General a long stare with his squinty eye, his mouth a hard line, not clear if he was playing along or was pissed. Then he turned back to Stef. "You see that rifle on the wall over there? That's my Model 70. Brought it back with me after V–J Day. First thing I did was go out hunting, up on Hel's Hill."

Everyone at the table had quieted down and was listening.

"Back then most of these hills were bare. Clear cut or burned off. I saw this sumbitch across the hollow, 300 yards. But that Model 70, she don't miss. By the time I hoofed it over there, there was blood, but no buck. So I started trailing him."

Doc came past and filled Finn's glass with a splash of whiskey.

"A storm came up. Blizzard. I had to spend the night curled up, tryna keep a fire lit. The coyotes were howling. I'd be damned if they was gonna get to that deer before me."

Finn took a sip, and continued. "Next morning, that sumbitch crossed the main road over into Crooked Creek. But there was snow and there was tracks. All day, from the base of Hel's Hill all the way up Crooked Creek hollow to the Shawmut Grade, I tracked him. A bit of blood here, a bit there. Maybe I just nicked him in the ear. Kept gettin' close, he kept just far enough ahead, couldn't get a clean shot. So the sun was getting low and goddamn if that sumbitch didn't cross the grade into North Fork. Signs posted all over the place 'No Trespassing.' The goddam Thiassens' land."

He looked over at Karl Thiassen and winked with his good eye.

"So I truss-passed. Was at the top of the cliff face lookin' down into this spring right out there. And sure enough there he stood, looking up at me." He held up his arm as if slowly lifting a rifle, crooked his elbow, and mimed a trigger pull with his finger.

"We heard the shot up at Frost Hall," Karl Thiassen jumped in. "Well, back then it was Frost Camp, a hunting camp like any other, a log cabin that my grandfather built himself. Me and the boys came down, and there was Finn looking all wild and ornery, gutting the deer. And what a deer. Twelve point."

Finn pointed his finger like a dart to the head mounted above the fireplace—the neck and head so massive, the rack so wide, it almost looked fake.

"I called out to Finn, 'You realize this land is posted and you are trespassing. That deer belongs to me.' And Finn put a hand on that M70 and said 'The hell it does.'"

Finn glanced around the table as if to a jury, palms up, pleading his defense.

Karl Thiassen continued. "As they say, we had reached an impasse. So, I made him a proposal. I asked him what he did before the war, and he told me he worked as a carpenter. Built houses. As it so happened, I had need of a carpenter. I had ideas of expanding the old log cabin into something … grander. And good men were hard to come by back then."

He reflected on that, then added, "Still are."

Karl Thiassen smiled at Finn, warmly placed a hand on his shoulder. "So we struck a deal right then and there, standing over that dead buck. Finn would build me Frost Hall, and in return he could have this plot of land that we're sitting on. His outright, I'd sign the deed over to him."

"And I could keep the deer," Finn added.

"Best business deal I ever made."

There was applause around the table, and Stef realized they probably told this same story, at this same table, to this same audience, every year.

People resumed eating, side conversations started up, and the noise level increased. Karl Thiassen was regarding Stef.

"Your dad told me you are pretty good with an axe. Which I like to hear! You know my company was founded way back by men who were good with axes."

Stef had a mouthful of steak, chewing, and could only nod.

"Your dad also told me about the university. That is quite an accomplishment. Congratulations." He raised his whiskey glass.

"I sent my sons off to college, too," he said. "Figured they would learn business, management, take over from me someday. All except my youngest, that is. Jessie—these boys here all called him 'Thunderbird'—he had the wild in him. He barely liked setting foot in town, let alone on campus …"

"God rest his soul," Finn mumbled.

"Thing is, they never came back. Oh sure, they worked summers at the powder-metal plant, or laying gas pipeline, or at the paper mill. But they never cared much for getting their hands dirty. They met girls and got jobs at big companies, had families. Now one lives in DC, one in New York, one in San Francisco. When they take vacations, it's to places like Aspen, the Caribbean, or Europe. Not that I blame them. It can get bleak here in the winters."

Oscar, who hadn't said a word yet, grunted.

"You see, I have a different philosophy. You know, my ancestors, they believed the whole world was made from the blood and bones of an old frost giant."

Finn looked uncomfortable at this turn of conversation and glanced over at the crucifix hanging above the front door.

"The land is wild and rough, but was put here for us to live on and—if we respected it—would nourish us."

Karl Thiassen made a gesture and Doc came over with a shot glass, set it down in front of Stef, and filled it with whiskey.

"I owe your family a great deal," he said. "Back during the Depression, it was your grandfather at the Savings & Loan who kept our business going through the leanest years when we thought we'd have to sell everything. Never foreclosed on us. Said it made more business sense to keep Thiassen making payroll …"

"And your dad. Don't let him fool you, he is as sharp a lawyer as you can find in any big city. He was working for the Mellons down in Pittsburgh, but chose to come back here. To raise *you* out here."

"First year back," he continued, "your dad comes up to me with the brilliant idea of putting all the Thiassen land into conservancy. An irrevocable trust. Make it state game lands. Tax-free. With the right to take a certain amount of timber annually, to keep the forest healthy. None of those bureaucrats down in Harrisburg knew sam hill about black cherry back then. By board foot, it's now the world's most valuable tree, and now I've got the exclusive right to harvest it …"

"But even more important than that, he reserved the oil and gas rights." Karl Thiassen's eyes glowed from behind his thick glasses. "Now I'm sure you're thinking—like the pencil pushers down in Harrisburg—that the world's oil comes from places like Saudi Arabia. Yes, the easy oil was gone from here a century ago. But I'm here to tell you, this land we're sitting on, underneath it all is a slab of rock called the Marcellus Shale. Eons ago this country was marshes and bogs, and all that organic material was compressed and cooked into oil and natural gas, locked inside the shale here like little bubbles. All it's going to take is for some bright mind to figure out how to crack it, and we'll have more oil, more gas, than anyone can imagine."

All of this was way over Stef's head and he had zoned out a bit, more curious about the glass of whiskey in front of him.

"You met my grandaughter, Kathi?" Karl Thiassen asked. That snapped him to attention.

"Y-yes," Stef stammered. "I mean, we just were talking."

Karl Thiassen nodded, smiling. "I bet. She is a handful. When Jessie came back from one of his trips up North with a baby, some people in town thought maybe he snatched her … but it didn't take long to see she was her father's daughter. She's made quite a name for herself. It's good to have her home."

"I saw her a minute ago outside, but she never came back in."

"She's nice enough to make an appearance for her Pops. She's heard these war stories a hundred times. Most likely headed back up to her dad's old hunting camp, up on top of the mountain. That's where she likes to stay. Actually, not that far from where you got that wood yesterday …"

Karl Thiassen eyed him closely, and for a moment it seemed like the rest of the party had receded, just the two of them across from each other.

"Your dad also told me you are good at maps."

"I'm all right, I guess," Stef said. "I mean, I like to draw maps of where we go hunting … just doodling really."

"I have a proposal for you, Stef," he said. "I need men. Good men. The kind that know how to use an axe. You graduate from high school this spring? Take the summer, enjoy yourself. There's a job at Thiassen waiting for you next fall. A good-paying job, just ask around. If you want to keep making maps, you can help me survey all these hills. Before anyone else figures out what we've got."

Stef just stared at him. "I don't know what to say. The university is … it's a big deal. I got accepted early decision and everything."

He looked over at the fire, pictured Skate standing in the cabin door.

"I mean, I'd have to talk to my parents."

Karl Thiassen said, "Of course. There is a lot to think about, and no rush. Let it soak. For now, let's take a drink." He nodded at the glass of whiskey, and lifted his own high. Stef looked around the table and realized all of the other men had shot glasses as well.

"Gentlemen!" Karl Thiassen proclaimed. "To the hunt!"

Stef downed the whiskey, trying his best to swallow in one gulp, but it caught in his throat and made him cough. Oscar put his hand on Stef's shoulder and said, "Second one goes down easier."

There were more stories, and coconut cream pie for dessert. Then the General checked his watch and stood up. It was time to leave. Stef did his best to avoid the Sauer twins' gaze as they made their goodbyes.

At the door on the way out, Doc came up to Stef and pressed something into his hand. It was a hunting knife, with a handle made from a deer antler, in a leather sheath. "Hobby of mine," Doc said, winking. "Have a machine shop behind the garage."

He patted Stef on the arm. "Good luck on Monday."

By the time they got back in the truck, Stef's head was spinning. He slumped back and looked out at the headlights cutting through the trees, casting lurching shadows. They swung past Frost Hall, lit up and dazzlingly bright.

"Well that does it," his old man said, listening to the static. "Notre Dame won." He switched off the radio and they drove the rest of the way to Hilo in silence.

SUNDAY

After breakfast, they drove up to sight in the rifles at the Sportsmen's Club. The club was located at the base of Hel's Hill, just around the bend from where Oscar lived, on the way back toward town. The sky was a clear blue dome overhead, the morning sun glinting sharp and diamond-like, making Stef's eyes wince from the after-effects of the party.

The family Olds was idling in the upper lot by the skeet-shooting range—a covered awning, a railing, and a little concrete pillbox that ejected clay pigeons out into a fan-shaped field. Seeing the vehicles coming down the hill, his mom got out, still wearing pajamas under a long winter coat and a pair of boots. The truck pulled alongside and Stef got out so he wouldn't have to sit in the middle.

In the woods beyond it sounded like a pitched battle was underway, one booming rifle shot after another.

His kid brother came over and wedged a duffle bag and a special pillow for his allergies in the space behind the cab seat, gave his mom a little hug, then climbed in the truck.

His mom turned to Stef. "Be nice to JR. Don't tease him."

"I won't, Mom."

"We never got to talk about the letter—"

He cut her off. "Not now."

She continued anyway, "—but I just wanted to say, how proud your father and I are of you."

"Mom."

"Okay, okay. I'll let you get back to your hunting. I have a good feeling this is your year, honey. You'll get that buck."

"Don't jinx it, Mom!"

She stepped forward and gave him a hug and he let her kiss him on the cheek. Then she walked around the front of the truck and gave his old man a peck too. "I think we've got everything," he said to her.

From the station wagon, the driver's window rolled down, the General leaned out, cleared his throat. "Marie, a few things …"

"Make sure you've got a spare tire for the truck. And remember the Olds spare won't work even if Jack says it will … " That had happened one year.

"If we don't phone up to town by 1900—thats 7 p.m. your time—send the game wardens up to South Fork with a can of gas …" That had happened another year.

"If Jack gets a buck—but 'twists his ankle' —be ready to come help drag it out …" That also had happened.

"If Jack loses his glasses, say a prayer to St. Anthony in hopes he will find them." That happened too, and she did, and he had found those glasses after all.

His mom gave a mock salute. "Women's Deer Auxiliary, at your service!"

They parted ways. His mom planned to spend the day with several of her fellow hunter's widows, driving to the nearest town that had a shopping mall—about an hour away—to get some Christmas deals.

They drove past the Sportsmen's Lodge and the trout hatchery pools where fry and fingerlings were raised, around the fishing pond and the picnic pavilion, across the main field used for parking, to an access road that led back to the shooting range, the constant hammer of guns now impossible to ignore.

The range was a large, tin-roofed awning and ten shooting benches spaced out evenly underneath. Trucks and cars could park in front of the stalls, and about half of them were occupied. The range faced outward across a large rectangular clearing of mowed grass cut out of the forest, mostly flat for the first hundred yards, but then the hillside tilted up sharply, rising like a wall and forming a natural backstop to fire into. There were signs painted with the distance, starting at twenty-five yards and going all the way up to 450, and wooden frames to hold targets placed at various depths.

They found an open spot near the middle and backed the cars in, opened the tailgates and spread out the gear: the encased rifles, boxes of ammo, and an old beer case filled with sandbags, paper targets, thumbtacks stuck in a piece of cardboard, scope covers, soft cloths, binoculars. His old man distributed squishy little foam earplugs that helped dampen the crescendo.

Mac had a big thermos and poured coffee into paper cups as they waited. Stef wandered over and examined a large bulletin board which posted the rules of the range, a map of hiking trails, as well as flyers for upcoming events: the ice fishing derby at the dam, the coyote hunt in February, trout stocking in April.

"All clear!" came the shout, and then up and down the firing line it was repeated. "All clear! … All clear! … All clear!"

The General took the old 30-06 over to the T-shaped shooting bench and arranged the sandbags while Stef walked with his kid brother out to the fifty-yard mark and pinned two targets side by side. At the other brackets, men were pointing, discussing shot patterns, and putting up new targets. One guy was huffing it all the way out to the 450-yard target, set high on the slope.

Everyone made it back to the shooting benches and once again the all-clear signal was shouted and echoed. A few moments later, the barrage resumed.

The General chambered a shell, leaned forward, adjusted his rear on the bench, was still for a moment, and then fired. As much as he knew it was coming, Stef found it hard not to flinch when the shot boomed.

"Six o'clock, an inch low," Mac said, looking through his binoculars.

The General nodded, went through the same routine, fired another round, spent a moment afterward peering through his scope, then ejected the shell.

"Same spot," Mac said.

Now they huddled around the bench and there began a consultation, as if preparing for surgery.

The General unscrewed the lids from the turrets.

"The top one is vertical," Mac said, giving the General guidance. "And the scope is one-quarter inch at a hundred yards … the target is at fifty … the shots are an inch low … which would be four clicks at 100 … so that needs to be eight clicks at fifty … up, which is clockwise."

"Isn't the shot rising at fifty yards?" his old man asked. "Don't you need to bring it up even higher?"

This went back and forth for a while and Stef tried to do the math in his head and quickly gave up. Finally, Mac fished a quarter out of his pocket, put it into the notch on the dial and counted out the clicks as he turned the coin. "Eight," he said, definitively.

They all stepped back and the General went through the same sequence, squeezed the trigger.

"You're there," Mac said. The General gave a nod, emptied the chamber, collected his brass, and dropped them into a tin pail at the base of the bench. As he came back over to the car, he rubbed his shoulder. "Still kicks like a mule."

"We got a lot of deer with that gun," his old man reminded him.

Next up was Mac who unbuckled the clasp on a hard case and removed his 30-30 lever-action rifle from the cushioned foam interior. With an economy of motion, he set up, chambered a shell, exhaled, and fired.

"Bullseye," the General said.

He loaded another round, aimed, fired.

"Bullseye," the General repeated.

Mac nodded once, and just as efficiently cleaned everything up and replaced the gun back in its protective case, went back to the station wagon and took a sip of steaming coffee.

"Remember that year we were loading up the car in the dark and someone dropped Mac's 30-30?" his old man almost had to shout to be heard through the earplugs and over the gunfire.

"You dropped the gun, Jack," the General reminded him.

"Allegedly," he replied. "That morning Mac missed three bucks by 10 a.m. We later discovered the scope was off by thirty inches at thirty yards."

"Why I bought the hard case," Mac said.

Mac had finished so quickly there was still time during this round of shooting, so his old man unzipped his rifle from its case—the "new" 30-06 that had been his since a teen way back in the 50s.

"I'll use the one on the right," he said to them. Mac had been so precise it might as well have been a clean target.

He went through his set up and spent a bunch of time fidgeting with the sandbags. Finally he settled in, wiggled a few times, adjusted his head in relation to the scope, then exhaled loudly. *BLAM!* The rifle kicked back and his old man noticeably flinched.

"Just outside the black ring, 9 o'clock," Mac reported.

His old man was shaking his head. When he turned in profile there was blood on his face. He touched the bridge of his nose. "Darn scope clipped me when the gun kicked," he said.

The General fished around inside the beer case, came out with a tin of bandages, and tossed it over. This was not the first time this had happened. The Yeager nose. *Aquiline*, as his old man like to describe it. Stef had been lucky enough to take after his mom's side.

He motioned Stef over to help him apply the bandage. There was a tiny, crescent moon-shaped cut on the left side of his nose with a dot of blood welling up.

In the meantime, the firing had petered out and the all-clear call came down the line. "All clear!" the General shouted in response.

"Where was the shot again?" his old man asked him.

"To the left," Stef said, standing over him, trying to get the angle of the bandage right before pressing down. "Just outside the center."

"Well I guess that proves the gun still works ..." he said. "Will have to be good enough."

He ejected the empty shell, made sure the safety was on, then stood up and took the rifle back to the car. Neither the General nor Mac said anything.

Most of the other hunters were out by their targets already, some headed back, and at a glance in that direction from the General, Stef and his kid brother quickly marched back out and replaced the used targets with fresh ones.

Now it was Stef's turn. His gun was a 308-caliber Mohawk 600 with a snub-nosed barrel—noticeably shorter than most deer rifles—a walnut stock with checkered chevron patterns along the forestock and grip, and a gold-plated trigger. No one ever explained exactly where it came from or why it was in the Yeager's gun cabinet. All of the other guns had some origin story, but not the Mohawk. When Stef started hunting at twelve, it was light enough for him to carry and it just became his. JR, on the other hand, got a brand-new Remington Model 700 from Hammerschmidt's on his twelfth birthday.

Sitting at the shooting bench, Stef opened the box of shells, took one out and peered at the tiny type around the brass rim to make sure 308 was printed there. He made sure the safety was on, and slid back the bolt, opening up the breech. He pressed the bullet down into the spring clip of the magazine until he felt it catch, slid the bolt forward just a tad, to make sure the action grabbed the shell, before continuing the motion forward, chambering the round, and locking the bolt down.

He tried to prop up the sandbags but they weren't cooperating, the top one slid off when he tried to rest the stock on top. The sandbags were situated right where his left hand would naturally hold the rifle, so he wasn't sure if he should reach around front or squeeze in his elbow tight to his side. Both felt awkward. He picked the latter, but felt all twisted up.

He closed his left eye and looked through the scope. At first he saw nothing but black, adjusted his head until the lens view swam into vision. It took him a few glances up from the scope and then back through the lens until he located the target in the crosshairs. At rest, the crosshairs were set up well to the right of the black bullseye and he had to squiggle the stock to get it lined up. But even then when he relaxed, the bullseye slid sideways, so he had to maintain a steady grip to keep in in place. He became very conscious of his breathing, the whole world narrowing down into the tunnel of the scope sight. With each breath, the crosshairs drifted about the target, not sitting still.

Then he remembered the safety was still on, and feeling around with his thumb, clicked it forward, ready to fire. He got the target lined up again, took a deep breath, and put his finger on the trigger …

And felt a hand on his shoulder.

"Not clear yet," the General said quietly.

Stef looked up and saw the guy from the 450 yard target was still making his way back, about twenty-five yards out. Not in his line of fire. But still. A wave of cold sweat broke over him.

"All clear!" came the call as he made it back to his bench.

"Thanks," Stef mumbled, looking up, but the General had already stepped away.

He started up the routine again, his heart now hammering, the earplugs making it sound like a roar, so loud he was sure others could hear. He located the target, and now the crosshairs were dancing across the bullseye: left, right, up, down. He did his best to remain steady, but that just made it worse. Finally, he just tried to time it as the crosshairs swept across the bullseye, and pulled the trigger.

He didn't hear the shot as much as felt the rifle butt bite hard into the bone in the hollow of his shoulder, and a sudden ringing in his ears.

"Down and to the left. About six inches. On the edge of the outer ring," Mac reported, looking through the binoculars.

"Take another one," his old man said.

Stef ejected the shell from the breech, fumbled another bullet out of the box, inserted it into the clip, and slid the bolt shut. He leaned forward and the sandbags were even more wobbly than before. He didn't hear any other shots—just the ringing and the sound of breathing and the pounding of his pulse—like everyone had stopped and was now watching him.

Again the crosshairs jumped around the bullseye, again he struggled to keep it steady long enough to pull the trigger. It seemed like a full minute passed. Finally, he saw the target line up for an instant, closed his eye, and squeezed the trigger.

Bam!

He looked through the scope to see where the shot had landed but the lens view was of pale straw, the grass off to the side of the target. There was silence from behind him, Mac not calling anything out.

"I think it slipped off the sandbags," Stef said.

"Mac," his old man said. "Would you mind helping out?"

Mac nodded once, came over to the shooting bench. Stef stood up and let him take his place, stepping back but still standing near the table. He watched as Mac methodically went through his routine, leaned forward, and after the briefest of pauses, fired a round.

"Just left of center," the General said. "In the black."

"That's good," his old man said.

Mac looked at Stef, saw the expression on his face. "Let me take another," he said.

He fired another round and this time it took a few seconds before the General responded. "It's left … well left. Down and to the left."

Mac said, "You know, the darn sandbags shifted on me." He stood up. "But that first shot it was solid."

He glanced over just briefly at Stef who was staring at him.

"Good gun," Mac said, handing it back to him.

Stef cleaned up the shells, got the rifle back in its case, and then hung back at the side of the truck while his kid brother set up. His old man was over at the bench, thumping the sandbags to ensure they were immovable.

Both of JR's shots were in the black.

~⊙⊙~

They followed the station wagon on the dam road, creeping along, weaving to miss the divots in the dirt road. Each year all of the camp owners raised funds to make improvements in the road—digging ditches, filling in sections with crushed gravel—and each year the weather methodically undid their work.

His kid brother was wound up, posing one question after another to his old man:

"Why can't deer see orange?"

"What's the longest shot you've ever made?"

"What's the exact time hunting starts and stops each day?"

"If you hit a deer and it doesn't go down right away, what do you do?"

"Are there really coyotes in the woods and what if you see one?"

Stef silently stared out the window, through the bare trees down to the lake glinting with sparks of the sun. They crossed the old bridge over Swamp Creek, rounded the hairpin turn, and continued down the last stretch of road. His old man pulled off in front of the Sauer's camp while the station wagon continued around the bend, onward to Hilo.

"Dad, no!" Stef cried out. "Why can't we just head back to camp?"

"Just a few minutes."

When his old man got on a roll telling stories, a few minutes quickly became an hour.

"JR, I think Kyle and Kenny are here." That got his kid brother's interest.

They climbed up the embankment on a rickety set of wooden stairs. Along the side of the camp, about half of the kegs were kicked and lay scattered on their sides. The flag hung limp on the flagpole. A few men loitered on the front porch and grunted hello as they passed.

Although it was noon and sunny out, inside the camp was dark and smoky and stank of men who'd been in tight quarters for many days. On one side of the door was a coat rack full of blaze-orange coats with licenses pinned to the back, and on the other side, a gun rack laddered with a dozen rifles. A sign was posted: *Hunting Tip #1: Must leave camp to get deer.*

A listless fire burned in the hearth and the twang of country music played on a radio. There were easily a dozen men inside the cramped space, maybe more. In the kitchen area were two fridges, one for food and one with a keg inside and a pull-handle tap jutting out of the side. The curtains were all drawn, and a tiny window over the sink provided the only light from outside, casting a tiny bright square on a pile of dishes and only serving to make the rest of the camp seem even darker.

Fred Sauer, standing there by the sink, saw his old man enter.

"Jack!"

He filled two red plastic beer cups from the keg-er-ator, one for his old man and the other one offered to Stef, who waved it off, so Fred kept it for himself. They clinked plastic in a toast. Meanwhile JR vanished into the shadows, looking for his friends.

"How are things down at the plant?" his old man asked.

Fred tugged at his beard. "It's been rough. More and more of the business is being shifted overseas. Most of our old competitors have gone tits-up. Now it's all Chinese."

"Karl Thiassen won't fold."

Fred nodded. "He's got us working on other things. Steel pipe. He's hoarding steel pipe. And sand. You ever been to Wisconsin? There's a lot of sand in Wisconsin, believe it or not. Some special kind, quartz, perfectly round grains like little bubbles." He rolled his fingertips together for emphasis. "Used to be part of a great inland ocean, back when there was dinosaurs."

"We drove out there last week on a tour of these open-pit sand mines," Fred continued. "It was hunting season in the state and Mr. Thiassen got us a guide. Man, the bucks are big out there. Corn-fed. The twins had a wrestling meet in Chicago and then joined us. Cole got a nice eight point."

"I saw the contracts," his old man said. "Looks like Thiassen's going on a buying spree."

"He gets crazy notions in his head. Keeps talking about 'The Marcellus,' that he just needs one breakthrough and it will be the return of the glory days." Fred took a long gulp of beer. "I dunno."

"I wouldn't bet against Karl Thiassen," his old man said. "He takes the long view."

"It's not him I'm worried about. He's getting up there, Jack. Who's gonna follow? Not those boys that moved off to the city. They are going to want to cash out."

His old man shook his head, "Thiassen's got it all wrapped up in a trust. Can't be sold."

"Jessie understood," Fred remarked. "Yeah, he was wild and crazy, but his word was iron."

"When I was district attorney, can't tell you how many times they brought him in. Poaching. There wasn't anyone who could take a deer from being shot to being cut up in the freezer faster than him."

"Remember that police spotlight he had mounted on his old T-bird?"

They both fell silent, drinking their beers.

"Ten years," Fred said, shaking his head. "Can you believe it?"

"He would have turned fifty this year."

"Nice to see his daughter at Finn's. Last time I saw her she was just a skinny girl with pigtails. Not anymore ..." Fred squinted out the window.

"Do you think she's back for good?" Stef asked.

They both looked at him, like he had suddenly appeared in their midst.

"Would answer a lot of your questions," his old man said to Fred.

Fred nodded. "And raise a whole set of new ones—"

Just then someone shouted out "Shhh! Forecast!"

Everyone quieted down and the volume on the radio got turned up.

... Accu-Weather forecast for Monday: Rain in the morning turning over to snow. High 36. Low overnight, 5 degrees ...

The radio broadcast switched over to news headlines, the volume was turned back down, and conversations started up again.

"Sounds like it's going to be a wet and wild one," Fred said.

"Reminds me of '81 when the first day there was a cloud burst," his old man said. "The General thought he missed a six point in the rain, no blood. But I found it at Christmas …"

"Wasn't that the year you brought a baby-buggy to haul your deer out?" Fred asked.

"I was the envy of all hunters."

Stef had heard these stories a hundred times and quickly lost interest. He asked if there was an indoor bathroom and Fred pointed him to the far corner of the camp.

He wedged past a card table with six guys seated in a circle of weak yellow light, cast from a lampshade hanging from a ceiling beam overhead. It looked like they had been there since the night before, grim expressions of distrust and exhaustion all around. Now that his eyes had adjusted to the gloom, he noticed the bunks stacked up to the ceiling, much like the gun rack by the door. His kid brother had found his classmates, who were hanging like bats up near the rafters, looking at a battered Playboy magazine from the 1970s.

As he approached, he saw the Sauer twins were there, wearing matching hoodies from Penn State, playing darts. The dartboard hung on the outside of a door, which opened with a tiny crack of light. A voice inside shouted "All clear?" and they yelled "All clear!" in response. Quickly a man ducked out, pants still unbuckled, revealing a closet-like bathroom, just big enough for a toilet.

Stef decided he could hold it.

"Hey, look, it's Steffi," one of the Sauer twins remarked.

"C'mon over and join us," said the other.

The tone in their voice was syrupy and friendly sounding, but he could see their eyes glowing red, reflecting the embers of the fire.

"Chew?" one of them asked, offering a pouch, the other spitting a string of brown juice into a plastic cup for effect. Stef shook his head.

"How 'bout a drink?"

On a side table was a bottle of Southern Comfort and a two-liter of cola. Without waiting for his response, they splashed a glug of each into a plastic cup, and extended it to him.

He looked over at the spit cup and couldn't tell them apart. *Could they have switched the cups?*

"No thanks," Stef said. "Still a little hungover from last night,"

"From *that* party?"

"Might as well have been a funeral wake, with all those old timers—"

"—but since you bring it up ... something we've been meaning to talk to you about—"

"—we saw Kathi Thiassen wave at you."

"She goes by Skate," Stef said.

They both laughed heartily.

"You actually think she's interested in ... *you*?!"

"A chick like that needs a real man."

"More like two men," more laughter, giving each other a high five.

"There we were, having a pleasant conversation with the lady, then you showed up—"

"—and that's the last we saw of her."

"Spooked like a doe."

"What, did you try asking her to the *prom*?"

"That girl's been around the world, if you know what I mean."

"Hey, toss that magazine down here so we can draw Steffi a diagram of what goes where."

Stef thought of saying something, then thought better, seeing the way their eyes were set, instead mumbled something inaudible, turned, and headed for the exit.

"Aw, don't get your panties in a twist!" they called after him.

He passed his kid brother who had overheard all that and was looking at him with moon eyes. His old man was holding court in the kitchen, gesturing, still in the middle of some old yarn.

"JR, tell Dad I'm walking back to Hilo."

Outside the sunlight was like a flashbulb and momentarily blinded him. He took a deep breath of crisp air, blinked, then rapidly walked down the embankment stairs and past the family truck without looking back. High overhead, wispy cirrus clouds had moved in and streaked the blue sky. The road was empty, his boots crunched on the gravel as he marched forward, around the bend, putting the Sauer camp out of view behind him.

It wasn't far to the turnoff to Hilo. He stood there at the top of the hill, looking down at the flat black rectangular roof of their camp, smoke rising from the chimney, the station wagon parked alongside, the stack of firewood and picnic table, and beyond, the gray-green water of the lake ruffled with a slight breeze, the thin strip of the dam breastwork just visible in the distance around the point of the cove at the end of the main channel.

The wind had a slight edge to it and his eyes were welling up. He jammed his fist into them, rubbed his sleeve across, to wipe them clear.

When Stef entered Hilo, there was a crackling fire burning in the fireplace. The angle of the afternoon sun slanted through the front picture windows and brightened everything. Mac was sitting in one of the lounge chairs, his legs propped up, feet in wool socks close to the fire, a steaming mug next to him on the side table.

Mac pointed to the closed door of the bedroom. "He's napping."

Stef nodded and, not knowing what else to do with himself, sat down in a chair across from Mac. The fire was just getting going, the clean cherry wood stacked in a neat crib, long orange flames leaping up from the kindling, lapping around the corners of the logs, singeing charcoal streaks along the edges.

A pair of vertical still life paintings hung above the fireplace, one showing dead muskies on a chain, the other dead pheasants strung up by their feet. To the left and right were pictures of a buck rubbing velvet off its antlers, another of a buck in full running stride, leaping across a fallen log. Along the other walls were trophy racks from years past and a framed photo of Stef's grandpa and grandma who built the place.

They sat in silence for a while, listening to the wood hiss and pop.

Then Stef said, "At the range today. Thank you."

Mac waved it off as nothing. "You know, right before you came in, I was just sitting here looking around. Thinking how much I like this place, like coming up here. It's a good place … not many places left like this."

Stef had never really thought much about it. The camp had always been here, the place their family went to.

"The first time I came up here," Mac said, "was when we had just got back from Vietnam …"

Mac looked into the fire as he talked.

"I was in command of an engineer battalion, we were attached to the First Cavalry Division. Airmobile—meaning helicopters. This was the first time anyone had used a force like this. They called it First Air Cav," he pointed at the logo on the mug, a big yellow shield, a black diagonal strip and a black horse head in the upper right. "Your uncle was a lieutenant colonel at the time and served as the XO— executive officer. I had known him and your aunt for many years, as acquaintances, but that was where we really became friends …"

"My job was to build a base for the helicopters, up in the highlands. Had to clear the jungle and build landing strips to handle over 400 helicopters. Set up radio towers on top of the nearby hills. Because we had to keep the grass trimmed so short—so debris wouldn't kick up from the propeller wash—everyone called it 'the Golf Course.'"

Mac took a sip from his mug, leaned forward.

"So after about a month there, the North Vietnamese attacked a nearby Special Forces camp. Once that siege was broken, the Air Cav was deployed in a campaign in the hills to the west. The terrain was similar to here, actually—steep slopes, sharp valleys—but heavy jungle. Some of our engineers were attached to these units to clear the landing zones, remove traps. 'Seek and destroy,' they called those missions. Use the helicopters to pogo-stick from one location to another," he illustrated with his hands.

"One of the helicopter battalions dropped into a landing zone that—without knowing it—was surrounded by practically the entire North Vietnamese army. It turned into a complete ambush. And that triggered what was possibly the fiercest battles of the war. It lasted five days ..."

"It was an incredible round-the clock test of everybody. We used tactics that never were attempted before—mobile artillery, air support from fighter jets, calling in B-52 bomber strikes. All to get those troops back out. My engineers had to establish a water supply—there was no water at the LZ where they were pinned down—and bring it in by helicopter under enemy fire ..."

"It was the most casualties of the war up until then. Over 200 of our soldiers were killed, and 300 wounded ... and maybe five times as many North Vietnamese. Nobody came out of that battle the same as they went in. Your uncle, being part of command, he still hasn't ever talked much about it—even to me. Except to remember different men. He wrote a lot of letters to families ..."

The fire crackled and they sat in silence for a while, Stef having no idea what to say and Mac seeming far away, lost in his thoughts.

Then he resumed, "When our tour was over and we got back to the States, we were home about a week and your uncle phones me and asks me to come along deer hunting with him. Says his family has a cabin up in the Pennsylvania woods and his younger brother Jack—your dad—was a big hunter and would be our guide ..."

"Now I thought there was no chance our wives would be okay with this. It was right after Thanksgiving. But I think even with us being back, they ... they could tell. So my wife encouraged me to go ..."

"You know how you can only buy liquor in state stores here? Well it was so much cheaper to buy booze down in Virginia. When I got into your uncle's car, the entire trunk was clinking from the amount of whiskey he had bought. Back then the state police actually set up roadblocks to catch people crossing state lines—'Checkpoint Charlie' we called it—and wouldn't you know it, we got pulled over ..."

"Your uncle gets out of the car, starts talking to the state trooper, and soon enough realizes he knows the guy's younger brother, who was in the infantry in Vietnam. And your uncle talks about this kid and their hometown like he'd grown up there. The officer ends up shaking hands, saying 'thank you, sir', waves us through..."

"When we get up here, as we made our rounds about town, to different hunting camps, your uncle had me handing out bottles left and right. A very easy way to make new friends ..."

"So that's what started it. We've been coming up here every year since. Twenty years. Wouldn't miss it. I find, when I'm out in the woods, I just don't think about anything else. The rest of the world with all its cares vanishes ..."

"Now you, I'm sure you can't wait to get away. See the world ..." He looked over at Stef with his clear blue eyes. "I heard about the university. Well done."

The truck pulled down the driveway and parked in front. Doors opened and banged shut.

"Just don't forget about all this," Mac said.

They entered the camp in a bustle, his kid brother lugging his duffle bag, his old man saying, "Stef, can you help bring in the rifles?"

Stef got up and did as he was told. When he came back in from the sunporch, the door to the bedroom was open.

"Weather?" the General asked.

"Looks like we are in for it," his old man said. "Rain in the morning, switching over to snow. Up here maybe all snow."

"Wind?"

His old man nodded. "Lows in single digits Monday night. So a front is moving through."

"Bit of everything."

"Nothing we haven't been through before," his old man said.

Before dinner they played a card game called Cinch. Four players, two teams, partners sitting across from each other, like bridge. A point was given for capturing the high card, the low card, the jack in the bidding suit, and game —summing up all of the face cards of any suit, with an ace being four points, king three, queen two, jack one, and tens counting for ten points. High was usually an ace, low a two, but not all the cards were dealt out, so sometimes a king or a three might sneak in worth a point.

Each hand, six cards were dealt and the bids went around the circle once, with the player to the dealer's left getting the first bid, passing or bidding how many out of four possible points he thought the team could win. If a good hand was under-bid, the next player could bid more and seize the initiative. Not making the bid was called being set, meaning you subtracted the points from the team's score. And there was a special bid, called shooting the moon, which—if successful in getting all four points—eight were awarded, or taken away. First team to fifteen won the game.

The player with the highest bid declared the trump suit, and then everyone discarded all of the cards not in that suit, and drew extra to make six cards in their hand. This variant in the game was called Brockway, playing Straight meant keeping the cards as they initially were dealt. So, in Brockway there was a moment to see how many trump cards each person started with, but it was still a mystery as to what they might have picked up in the draw.

The play went clockwise, starting with the bidder. The players had to follow suit if they had it in their hand. If not, they could play any card in their hand, including a trump card. High card won, except the highest trump card beat everything else.

Stef was paired with the General against Mac and his old man. JR watched from over Stef's shoulder—which was annoying—and kept score with a pencil and scrap piece of paper.

Stef committed a series of blunders: bidding three without having the jack, not being careful with his tens and enabling Mac to make his two bid by winning game, not immediately playing his jack when the General led with an ace. The General did not like losing—at anything—and was clearly growing frustrated, but never said a word and took the run of bad luck and poor play stoically.

They were down fourteen to eight as Stef dealt what looked to be the final hand. He fanned open his cards and saw the ace, king, jack, seven, and four of hearts. When the bid came around to him, he declared, "I'm shooting it! Hearts."

The General's eyebrows shot up. He laid down all of his hand, meaning he had no hearts in support. Mac—sitting to Stef's left—kept one card, and his old man—to his right—kept four. Stef dealt out cards to fill in everyone's hand. He drew the ten of spades—a valuable card if it came down to game.

Stef led with the ace of hearts, a straightforward opening play that allowed a player—if they had valuable point cards—to safely offload them to their partner. Mac played a six of hearts, and the General played the ace of spades—a terrible sign—meaning he had drawn no extra trump cards. The ace would count four points toward game, but it also meant that was the best he could contribute. The scowl on the General's face was pronounced. His old man put in an eight of hearts, and Stef took one point for high card, but that was all.

He next led with the king of hearts, hoping perhaps Mac who had only one trump card at discard, had drawn a valuable card, and would have no choice but to play it. But Mac laid down the five of hearts. The General contributed a jack of clubs, signifying he was just about out of anything of value. And his old man discarded the nine of hearts.

Now Stef was in trouble. He had jack–seven–four remaining and the queen, the ten, and the low card were still out there. He led with the seven of hearts, and Mac added the three of hearts for possible low. The General added a worthless five of diamonds, and his old man used the opening to play the ten of hearts, winning the hand, grabbing the possible low card, and getting ten points toward game.

Trying to get rid of the lead, his old man led with a nine of spades, forcing Stef to follow suit with his ten of spades. Stef won the hand, and kept his ten toward game, but this was not a good thing, because the queen was likely still out there and now Stef had to lead. If he led the jack, the queen would take it and it would be game over.

So he played the four of hearts … and Mac played a diamond, meaning he was out of trump. When it came around to his old man, suddenly a frown flashed across his face. He looked at his last two cards, then over at Stef, and reluctantly played the queen of hearts.

The General, who had been glancing at his watch, suddenly sat up straight. His old man had no choice but to play his final card—the deuce—and Stef laid his jack down on top of it, capturing the low as well!

A quick tally of cards showed Stef had a ten, two aces, a king, a jack—twenty-two points—while his old man had a ten and a queen—twelve points.

Stef had pulled it off. He had shot the moon!

"With eight points ... the final score is sixteen to fourteen!" his kid brother announced, raising his arms above his head.

The General grinned from ear to ear, reached across to shake Stef's hand, looked over at his brother Jack, and winked, "Never in doubt."

His old man patted Stef on the shoulder and said, "Well played. I thought for sure you were trapped."

Stef stepped outside to get more wood for the fireplace. It wasn't even 5 p.m. and already the sun had set, lighting up the clouds that had rolled in from underneath in a diffused yellow-and-pink glow. He realized by the time the sun rose the next morning he would be out in the woods.

Stef thought to himself, maybe my luck is changing ...

After they had eaten dinner—spaghetti with the meat sauce his mom had made, plus garlic bread, and pumpkin pie with cool whip for dessert—cleared the table and washed all the dishes, they reassembled around the dining table. Mac poured them each a glass of blackberry wine from a twist-top jug, purplish and almost syrupy sweet. Even JR got a glass.

"Stef, why don't you bring out the map," his old man said.

Stef unrolled the topographic quad map on the table, with the lake colored in cheerful blue, the state forest in bright green, and the elevation gradients shown as squiggly brown lines—the closer the lines, the steeper the slopes.

"How about the one you drew?"

Stef was surprised at that, but went to his duffle bag and retrieved his hand-drawn map, which was carefully folded up inside a book.

Stef laid the map on the center of the table facing the men. The General spent some time examining it, glancing over at the topo map, consulting his memory. Then he looked at Stef and gave the briefest of nods.

"We'll dock the boat in the usual spot," his old man said, pointing to where South Fork flowed into the dam. "Then we'll follow the left bank of the creek upstream to Frigg's Hollow. The brook there should be running, we've had enough rain this fall..."

"Mac, you'll be up in the Pines ..."

The deer stand they called the Pines was in was an old patch of hemlocks just up a short side hollow, close quarters, but just the sort of place deer liked to mill about, especially in poor weather.

To the General, he said: "... and I thought you could head up to Spike Point ..."

Spike Point had a nice view down across a wide bench that was a natural path for deer heading toward the Pines. Now that the General and Mac were getting older, these spots weren't too far in, usually saw action the first day, and were pretty easy drags straight downhill to the boat. Not that either of them would ever admit it.

The General thought it over, again gave the slight head nod. That was important. It's not often a four-star general is assigned anything, let alone by his younger brother, but here at Hilo it was unquestioned—well, usually—that Jack was in charge of deciding who sat where.

"I'll take JR up to Blind Man's Hollow ..."

This was a big year for his kid brother, now old enough to stand watch by himself for the first time. In previous years he'd hunted alongside his dad, and Stef had stood at Blind Man's—which was given that name because one year, the General got a deer right at dawn and so they strung it up from a tree. Mac had come by and asked if they'd had any luck, with the deer dangling right above his head, practically dripping blood down on him.

" ... and Stef, from there you can continue on to Big Buck ... "

Stef could barely contain his surprise at the news. Big Buck Hollow was a prime hunting spot. The name spoke for itself. The stand was usually reserved for his old man, who had lots of success there over the years, including the last two for JR as his sidekick.

"… and after I drop off JR, I'll cross Frigg's Hollow to Bear Behind." So named because one year a big black bear was spotted up on the flats behind the stand. It wasn't a great stand compared to the others, but if something came running down the main draw it offered a wide-open shot.

"We'll see what the action is like in the morning. If nothing's moving, around eleven, I'll circle through the edge of the Slashings to see if I can move anything."

The Slashings were an old clear cut which had grown up with blackberry briars and pencil-thin saplings clustered so dense it was almost impossible in places to walk through, and very easy to lose your bearings once in them. The deer, though, had no problem moving about and liked to vanish into the Slashings if spooked.

"What time is first light?" the General asked.

Stef took out the *Hunting & Trapping Digest*, a booklet of rules and regulations that came with the hunting license, and located the date on the hunting hours table. The starting time was listed as 6:37 a.m., which was thirty minutes before sunrise. But each meridian west of the seventy-fifth added four minutes to the start time. On the map, they were past the seventy-eighth meridian, or plus-twelve minutes.

"6:49 a.m." Stef announced.

"If there's weather there won't be much of a sunrise," his old man added. "It's a new moon, not that that will matter either. And no snow. Meaning, as soon as you can see, the season will have started."

"Let's work backward," the General said.

"Okay. We're going to want to be in our spots a half hour before first light."

"0620," the General said.

"Stef's got the longest walk in, about thirty minutes. Let's say forty to be safe. And ten minutes getting out of the boat."

"South Fork landing 0530," the General said.

"About a twenty-minute boat ride in the dark. Add ten minutes getting down and into the boat."

"Leave Hilo 0500."

"And maybe an hour getting up and ready here."

"Wake up 0400."

"Breakfast," Mac pointed out.

"Okay. Set the alarm for 0345," the General said with finality.

Stef knew for sure that all three of them would be up at 3:30 a.m.

In agreement on the plan, they broke from the table, went to their sleeping spots, and began to prep their gear for the morning. The General and Mac were in the bedroom, his old man and kid brother were in the little sleeping nook to the right of the front door, and Stef had the couch in the main room near the fireplace.

Stef brought a chair over that he could use to arrange everything. He worked from outside-in, in reverse order of how he'd get dressed in the morning.

First came the hunting coat. He started with the license holder attached to the back of the coat by an oversized safety pin. The clear plastic panel displayed his license, printed on shiny silver card stock. He made sure it was signed and was the current year—it was easy to forget and accidentally use last year's—the license colors from year to year were minor variations of gold, copper, silver. Unless of course you got a deer and had torn off the deer tag, the perforated bottom third of the license—that was pretty obvious. He also checked inside the holder for a golf pencil—used to fill out the deer tag—and a sandwich bag twist tie to fasten to the deer's ear.

In the game pouch at the rear of the coat—accessed by two vertical buttoned pockets on either side—he put in about six feet of drag rope and a pair of surgical gloves for gutting the deer. He also added a folded-up orange rain poncho, hoping against hope he wouldn't need it.

In the right front cargo pocket he placed the cartridge holder, a plastic sleeve that held ten bullets, after first examining each one to make sure stamped with 308 and that none of them were visibly corroded. Ten shells was plenty. If you need more than ten shots, maybe you weren't meant to get the deer.

He put two new double-A batteries in the mini flashlight, checked to make sure the beam was strong, then stashed the flashlight in the front left cargo pocket as well as four pouches of hand warmers, two for the morning and two for the afternoon. He also tucked a big bulky ski glove into each pocket, as well as thin cotton shooting gloves that he could wear if there was action.

In the left breast pocket, he placed a compass, and in the right, a box of matches wrapped in aluminum foil to keep dry.

Once the hunting coat was loaded up, he hung it on a hanger on the coat rack by the front door alongside the other coats, ready to put on right as they headed out. He propped his hunting cap—blaze orange with warm earflaps that could be folded down—on the shelf above, next to the General's classic red wool hat.

On the chair seat, he placed his coiled leather belt, a digital watch, and a plastic whistle on a lanyard that he would wear around his neck, used for blowing signals to each other. One whistle meant *Where are you?*, two whistles was the response *Here I am*, three whistles meant, *Come right away I need help*, and four whistles meant *I got a deer.*

Alongside he laid the new hunting knife that Doc had given him. He liked the way the bone handle felt in his grip. The leather sheath had a little arrow-circle-and-stars Thiassen brand burned into it that he hadn't noticed before. They probably gave these out as mementos to the guests at Frost Hall. He unbuckled the snap and slid the knife out. The blade was short, curved, and sharp.

On top of these items he stacked his folded gray wool pants, which were perfect for hunting. They were warm, could absorb a lot of water, and didn't make a swooshing sound like snow pants did when walking, which could easily spook deer. Then a red flannel shirt, heavy long underwear tops and bottoms, a thin down vest to provide extra warmth, and a balaclava scarf that could be pulled up as a face mask if it really got cold.

He had two pairs of socks—a thin, almost stocking-like bottom layer to wick away sweat, and a thick woolen sock to go on top and provide warmth. These went into his muck boots, which were green rubber on the bottom with camouflage neoprene uppers that went all the way to the top of his calves. These were step-in boots—no zippers or laces. They had experimented with all kinds of boots over the years and decided these were the best for nearly any and all conditions.

He looked over all his gear one last time, satisfied. He was as ready as he could be.

In the kitchen, Stef helped Mac make lunches for everyone— ham and cheese sandwiches on whole wheat bread with mayo and mustard, kept in folded sandwich bags so they wouldn't fall apart, a macintosh apple, a handful of bite-sized candy bars, a sports drink— all placed together into gallon-sized zipped plastic bags that fit snugly in the game pouch at the rear of the hunting coats. Mac filled hip flasks with blackberry wine, including one for Stef.

He waited his turn for the bathroom and, by the time he finished, the lights in the camp were turned down low. The General was already in bed. He said goodnight to Mac, then JR and his old man, who were getting the alarm clocks set up, double-checking against a watch and the clock in the kitchen. Roughly 10:15 p.m. They set two different clocks, a digital clock with glowing red numbers and a klaxon alarm, and a wind-up clock with a bell ringer that would act as a backup if the power went out during the night, which had happened one year during an ice storm and everyone overslept.

He rolled out his sleeping bag on the couch and cracked open his book and tried to read for a while. *The Hobbit.* He re-read the same line several times, spent some time looking at the treasure-map with the dragon in Lonely Mountain, then closed the book and clicked off the lamp.

The fire was burning down to coals but still sending up flickers of yellow flame that cast long, jumpy shadows, the racks of antlers projecting a trembling web across the ceiling, a soft hiss and crackle, the drone of the refrigerator, muffled snoring coming from the bedroom, more of a loud saw coming from his old man in the alcove.

He closed his eyes, curled up tight inside his sleeping bag, and tried to empty the thoughts racing through his head. He pictured the fire at her cabin, her turquoise necklace, her sleeping bag rolled out on the bunk in the corner, the shape of her standing in the doorway, the way the fire caught her eyes ...

He looked at the wall clock in the kitchen. The minute hand had barely budged—10:30 p.m.

Overhead he heard the first patters of rain against the roof.

MONDAY

From a dreamless, blank sleep he dimly became aware people were up and moving about. He heard shuffling in the kitchen, the crisp bite of coffee being scooped, the tap running and water filling up the glass pot, then being poured into the coffee maker, the rumble and glug and drip as it brewed, the smell of coffee filling the camp. Pans rattled against the electric coils on the stove top, the sizzle and hiss of sausages, the paper-thin crack of eggs and whisk of them being scrambled. He pressed his eyes shut and curled his body even tighter around the core of warmth in his sleeping bag, as if it were a ball he could cradle and cling to.

"Up and at 'em," his old man said, shaking his shoulder as always.

Stef groaned and sat upright on the couch, rubbed the sleep out of his eyes. Across the room in the alcove his kid brother was also sitting up in his sleeping bag, his hair all tousled, looking around dazed like he'd just tumbled down a hill.

The fire had gone out overnight and the wheezing electric heaters could only do so much. When his bare feet touched the floor, which was just carpet on concrete, it sent a shiver through him. He quickly wriggled into his long underwear bottoms and pulled on the matching top, tugged the thin stockings on, slipped the heavier wool socks on over top. But the cold had already seeped in, and the halo of warmth from the sleeping bag had vanished.

He used the bathroom, then came out and continued dressing. He put on his wool pants, with the knife belted to his hip, buttoned up his flannel shirt, fastened the wristwatch, slipped the lanyard over his head and tucked the plastic whistle in the breast pocket so it wouldn't jangle about, but left the down vest for after breakfast, not wanting to get too bundled up just yet and start to overheat and sweat. Mac was in the kitchen in his long johns putting the finishing touches on breakfast. Servings were doled out onto paper plates with wicker holders, mugs filled. Stef usually didn't drink much coffee, but this morning it was necessary. Everyone ate around the bar counter without much talking. The General wolfed down his food and coffee in an instant.

"Stef, see if you can get something on the radio," his old man said as the rest of them finished up. Mac was pouring the rest of the coffee pot into his thermos.

The radio was an antique the size of a toaster, sporting two big dials for tuning and volume, five polished keys like domino tiles. The vacuum tubes hummed when you clicked it on, casting a ghostly greenish glow around its front grill. On a perfectly clear and cold night, the radio could pick up shortwave broadcasts in French, Russian, and Japanese. Stef clicked the MW key, which was the AM band, fiddled around until he was able to tune in KDKA 1020 from Pittsburgh. None of the local stations came on the air until 5 a.m.

The broadcast was an overnight talk show where insomniacs and early risers called in and complained about politics, local issues, and various conspiracy theories. The weather and headlines came on every twenty minutes. The signal came in clear for a minute, washed into static, returned. A lady was explaining how she was certain her cat was trying to communicate something important to her.

Stef went to get the lunches from the sunporch where they had been stored overnight to keep cold. Rain tapped steadily against the roof, like pebbles scattering, the sound always magnified out here because the sunporch wasn't insulated. He tried to peer outside, but the windowpanes were black mirrors, coated with mist, reflecting the light from inside the camp and his shadowy image.

As he was carrying the armful of zipped plastic bags back inside, he realized he had forgotten to add paper towels, which could be used as napkins, to clean off scopes, mop up blood and—most importantly—as toilet paper. From the roll in the kitchen, he tore off an arm's length for each bag, folded them up, and resealed the plastic zippers, then went down the line of hunting coats and slipped lunch into everyone's rear game pouch. *That could have been a catastrophe.*

The clock read 4:40, and right on cue the radio host politely interrupted the cat lady's monologue and smoothly segued into news and weather. The reception was coming in and out as he read the forecast: ... *winter storm warning ... low forming off coast ... heavy snow ... gusts ... plummeting ...* Then the broadcast went to commercial.

Everyone had stopped what they were doing to listen, and now there were uneasy glances back and forth among them.

"It said coastal storm, so it could stay south and east of us ..." his old man said.

"The boat?" Mac asked, thinking of the time he almost fell in. "We could switch out plans and head to Hel's Hill instead ..."

"The road could be worse. That hill ..." his old man said, thinking of the time he hit black ice coming down Hel's Hill, slid off the road and nearly down the cliffside. Doc had to use the winch to get the truck up out of the ditch.

The General spent a moment considering, then said, "Stick with the plan. We go."

And that was that.

Stef zipped up his down vest, pulled the balaclava scarf over his head. On the dining table, his old man had spread out a half-dozen round waterproof cushions filled with styrofoam pellets, like beanbags. He clipped one to the back of his belt so it dangled over his rear end and would keep his ass dry if he sat down. He donned his hunting coat, which felt like it weighed an extra twenty pounds with all the gear in the pockets, and topped it all off with his hunting cap.

His old man had placed a box of scope covers at the corner of the bar counter, so they were hard to miss walking past. Stef fished around until he found ones that fit the Mohawk, optic yellow plastic lenses with a pair of elastic bands to keep them fastened, which he jammed into a front pocket on the way out to the sunporch. On the table among the other rifles, he made sure his case was zipped up so the rifle didn't slide out accidentally.

Then he went out the porch door and stepped into the night.

Drizzle fell, one notch up in intensity from a fine mist, cold and clammy, his breath in a wreath around his head as he stood on the driveway waiting for the others to assemble. His old man was the last one out, after making one last stop in the bathroom. The lights in the camp were all turned off except one lamp, left on for when they returned that night.

Stef took out his flashlight and shone it at the wooden railing at the top of the stairs that led down to the dock, streaks of rain fizzing through the beam of light. He led the way down, familiar since childhood with each of the stone steps that had been set into the hillside, could traverse them with his eyes closed. The flashlight was more for everyone else, and he shone it down at his feet so the cone of light directed backward a few feet for the General who was following him.

At the bottom of the stairs was an embankment down to the rocky shoreline. Their boots crunched on the gravel along a path JR had raked clear. Fog rose from the lake in slow, twisty columns, raindrops mottled the surface where the flashlight swung over, penetrating the dark green water just enough to indicate it was very deep, coming to rest on the dock and boat, which appeared tiny in the beam of light in comparison to the surrounding ocean of darkness.

At the ramp they waited on shore, lessons learned from years past. Stef held his kid brother's rifle case while JR climbed like a monkey, uncovering the boat, careful as he went so the pebbled water on the tarp rolled off the sides and he didn't get himself wet in the process. He rolled up the cover and stored it in the stern of the boat.

Next, his old man walked out the ramp tenderly, making sure the muck boots didn't slip on the boards. He stepped into the boat, stowed his rifle case carefully along the sideboard, and then he and JR worked in tandem, JR squeezing the fuel bulb to make sure there was enough pressure in the fuel line to the motor, his old man pulling out the choke and turning the key. A loud metallic whirring rang out for a few seconds, but the engine didn't start.

His kid brother went to squeeze the bulb again but his old man said, "Wait. Don't flood it."

There was pause as they all just stood there and the rain sprinkled down from the void.

His old man gave it another try, the shrill grating noise spun up again, shrieked … but just as Stef figured it was another dud attempt, the engine caught—a cough and a grumble and then a steady deep growl as a miasma of exhaust shrouded the outboard motor.

The lights came on, red and green in the bow and a white light on a tall pole at the rear starboard, pretty halos that did little but emphasize how thick the fog was.

That was their signal and, one by one, the General, Mac, and lastly Stef walked out onto the dock and climbed into the boat, JR kneeling up front holding the dock so the boat didn't drift as people stepped heavily aboard, the engine roaring furiously at full throttle on idle, his old man taking no chances of it stalling out. Stef sat down next to JR in the bow seats, placing the rifle cases securely in the seat well, thankful the dry seat cushion clipped to his belt came between his rear end and the already-damp boat seats.

His kid brother untied the bow rope and tossed it onto the dock and the General did the same in the stern. His old man made sure everyone was seated, backed the throttle down to a steady thrum, and shifted the engine into reverse. Once they were a good distance from shore, the boat started moving forward, picked up speed, and the running lights were switched off. No one else was out on the lake, and night vision made it easier to navigate. A barely perceptible line marked the solid black of the surrounding hills from the soft black of the sky above. The familiar shape and contour of the ridgelines were enough to triangulate where they were on the lake.

Sitting in the open bow, looking forward into complete darkness as the wind and rain and mist rushed by gave him vertigo, like the boat was about to plunge over the edge of the world into the abyss. He shut his eyes and turned his back to the breeze and stinging rain, huddled into a crouch, trying to preserve whatever bit of warmth he had carried with him from the camp.

He squinted over at his kid brother, who seemed to be enjoying the ride.

After a few minutes he started to shiver uncontrollably, and in a panic thought to himself that if he was feeling this cold already, on a short boat trip—already prepared to call it quits and turn back—how would he ever make it through the entire day?

Mercifully, the boat throttle cut back, the shrill whistle of the wind receded, and the whine of the engine was replaced by the plowing whoosh of the boat decelerating as it pulled into South Fork cove. Soon they were coasting forward under momentum, the motor purring on idle, the sound of their trailing wake crashing against the invisible shoreline.

His old man plugged the spotlight into the cigarette lighter and handed it to Mac, who was standing next to him with a steadying hand on the top of the windshield. The lamp beam shot forward like a lightning bolt, knifing a tunnel through the braids of fog. The boat drifted, now almost motionless, the spotlight like a pointed finger probing left and right. A dark angled strip emerged and Mac said above the grumbling engine, "Shoreline at two o'clock. Twenty yards."

His old man turned the wheel subtly, and the angle of the shoreline became perpendicular and grew, and now the shapes of tree trunks emerged further back in the cone of light. On one of the trees—a big old hemlock—a red reflector winked back at them.

"I see it," his old man said.

Mac focused the beam on a clear patch of shore, the boat floated in, and the bow crunched into the gravel. Stef and his kid brother hopped out of the front, splashing down into shallow water only a few inches deep, nothing the muck boots couldn't handle.

Stef tied one end of the waterskiing rope to the metal eyelet on the bow with two half-hitches, and JR paid out the line as he marched up the shore to the trees, Mac lighting the way for him. He wrapped the rope once around the hemlock. His old man raised the motor forward so the propeller was out of the water.

Stef went up and together with JR pulled on the rope, the three men now having shifted to the stern of the boat, their combined weight lifting up the bow just enough that the brothers could tug the boat another foot further ashore. Stef secured the end to the tree with another knot, then they marched back down to the shore.

The sequence of getting people and rifles off the boat was tricky. The General went first. He took the old 30-06 from its case and handed it down to Stef, then sat on the bow, feet dangling, and hopped down the last foot with JR assisting by shining his flashlight on the shore and providing a shoulder for the General to grab. Once ashore, Stef returned his rifle to him.

They repeated the same for Mac and his old man without incident. His kid brother climbed into the boat, unzipped the last two cases, and handed down their rifles one at a time. Stef held both, one on each shoulder, shining the flashlight while JR unfurled the tarp, working from stern to bow, and covered the boat back up. It was a struggle to get the tarp stretched taut, the buttons lined up and snapped shut, and as he ran out of real estate in the front of the boat, he just hopped into the shallows and finished the fastenings from the outside.

Stef found the burst of activity helped to dispel the chill he felt on the ride over. The rain was still falling as a steady drizzle, but the hat, coat, gloves, thick wool pants, and muck boots were doing their job. He was damp, but felt exhilarated to have the boat trip behind them.

They reassembled under the hemlock tree. Stef and his old man had their flashlights on and pointed directly down at the ground to avoid blinding anyone. They snapped covers over the lenses on the scopes. The heavy boughs of the hemlock blocked much of the direct rain, but fog and mist drifted past. Their orange coats and shouldered rifles were lit from below, puffs and halos of breath hovered around their heads. The General looked at his watch, little green luminescent hands on the dial.

"0545," he said. "Right on schedule."

A rumble came from over the opposite hill, and for a moment they all thought it was thunder. But a globe of light appeared up high near the ridgetop, then resolved into headlights, a convoy of at least a half dozen, lined up like a string of Christmas lights, bobbing and weaving and roaring down the hillside toward the end of the cove.

The Sauers crew.

They had given up on the boat ferry a few years back and now used ATVs, drove out the camp road, crossed over the breastwork of the dam, and picked up an old logging road that traversed the hump of the hill above the lake, running roughly parallel to the shore, then descended into South Fork cove. It was easily an hour ride that the boat covered in less than twenty minutes.

The Sauers usually hunted the main valley of South Fork and the hollows that branched off from it: Frey's Hollow, Hidden Hollow, Caskey's Draw. But you never knew with that crew. They could just as easily head up Frigg's Hollow by mistake and flood the zone with hunters. If on stand and another hunter came past, the rule was to flash a light and the latecomer would move on. But the finer points of etiquette might be lost on that bunch.

Stef could tell his old man was considering waiting for his buddy Fred Sauer to arrive with his twin sons so they could exchange a few words of good luck and maybe plan to meet up in the afternoon to put on a joint drive …

"C'mon lets get going!" Stef burst out.

The three men all stared at him.

"Yeah, I don't want to lose my spot!" JR said, seeing the look on his big brother's face.

Mac added, "The walk will help warm me up."

His old man saw where this was headed.

"Okay," he said, nodding. "Let's roll 'em out."

They formed up into a single file, his old man leading the way with his flashlight, followed by JR, the General, Mac, and Stef bringing up the rear, angling his flashlight down at their boots to illuminate the ground in between as they walked into the forest.

On the right, South Fork flowed past invisibly, about ten feet wide where it emptied into the lake. A steel and wood-plank bridge spanned the creek here, really the only formal crossing, though once you got a mile upstream it was shallow enough to cross on foot. A sign marked the boundary of state game lands and prohibited access by motor vehicle beyond.

Stef kept his eyes on the reflective tabs on the back of the muck boots, the oblong of ground lit up by his flashlight as it scrolled past, one step after another. South Fork was running with more urgency than usual from the overnight rain, the sound of the stream about equal to the sound of the rain falling through the trees. The rumble of the ATVs receded behind them.

A half-mile in, their flashlights shone across a broad swath of vividly green mossy stones and gurgling black water flowing down into South Fork, indicating they had reached the bottom end of Frigg's Hollow.

His old man turned them left and followed the trickling brook up into Frigg's Hollow along the last remnants of an old tram road, now all but absorbed back into the forest, with fallen trees and branches crossing the way at regular intervals that they had to step over—an effort in all the gear, but otherwise flat enough that it made the walking easier and provided a pathway to follow in the dark.

They came to a stand of old hemlocks and here his old man paused. They called this spot Headquarters. Because of its central location in the main hollow, it served as a good meeting point. Stef had fully warmed back up by now and was starting to sweat, unzipping his coat halfway to vent the steam from his chest. Mac was winded, but did his best not to show it. His old man and the General might as well have been strolling down the street to church, unaffected by the hike so far. His kid brother was like a puppy straining at the leash.

The fog was dense as cotton batting here in the hemlock grove, the pines acting like a natural comb catching the fog as it rolled in off the lake. It felt like the rain was tapering off, but it was hard to tell if that was just because they were standing underneath the pine boughs.

His old man shone the flashlight into the dense stand of trees, methodically going from trunk to trunk in the fog. Then a little spark winked back. He shone the light there again, wiggled the beam a little.

"You see that, Mac?"

Mac nodded. He had his flashlight out and shone it at the same location.

They exchanged wishes of good luck, and Mac walked up to the location of the first cat's-eye tack and shone his light into the pines, the same method his old man used, slowly scanning ahead, until his beam locked in on the next one. He looked back, gave a thumbs up, then followed the beam into the dense fog and immediately vanished into a ghostly glow, like a will o' the wisp drifting through the hemlocks.

The four of them continued on. A short side-draw opened up to the left past Headquarters and the tram road cut across the bottom of it. A big tree had fallen here since last year that was too much to climb over, so they had to work their way around the tangled earthen fan of the upturned roots. On the other side, his old man followed a phantom trail that ended in a tangle of branches, and they had to backtrack to the downed tree before picking back up the faint trace of the tram road. The General glanced at the glowing dials on his watch.

The rain had stopped, what still fell were scattered drops from the tall tree branches way overhead. It was noticeably a few degrees colder, the air still damp but freshened, and here beyond the pines there was no fog. When they reached the far side of the draw, two cat's-eye tacks glinted on the path ahead. From that point, shining the flashlight up and to the left, a line of little stars ascended the hillside like a staircase, pointing the way up to Spike Point.

The General propped a boot up on a log and rested his hand on his thigh, the other hooked into the strap of his shouldered rifle, looking up at the climb ahead—every inch a general, and at the same time, his age showing.

His old man gave his brother a questioning look, and the General wordlessly replied with a definitive nod. *Yes.*

"Good luck, men," the General said, clicked on his flashlight, and started up the steep slope.

The three of them didn't wait around and pressed onward. The old tram road was now little more than a foot path, in fact might have ended a ways back and it was just his mind playing tricks that they were actually still on a trail instead of just walking through the forest.

Past Spike Point another hollow opened up and branched off to the left, leading up to Blind Man's, and sure enough it was only a couple of minutes since they parted from the General that another pair of cat's-eyes glittered ahead of them.

"Here's the plan," his old man said in a whisper as they huddled.

He shone the flashlight off to the left, picking up the gleam of a cat's-eye about fifty yards away on one of the towering trees in the center of the hollow.

"I'm going to take JR up to Blind Man's ..."

He directed the beam straight ahead and after searching a bit found the cat's-eye, concealed behind a cluster of beech saplings, which were unique in that they kept leaves on branches all through the winter. The pale shriveled leaves reflected the light and made it hard to spot the reflective tack on the other side.

"Stef, your path lies straight ahead. It's going to dog-leg to the left, climbing up to a flat bench, then follows along that edge up to the head end of Big Buck Hollow."

"I know, Dad," Stef whispered back.

His old man shone the flashlight to the right and a little behind them. Several cat's-eyes dotted a path down to the creek. "Once JR is at his spot, I'm going come back through here and head up to Bear Behind."

He slanted his flashlight upward toward the invisible ridgeline on the opposite side of the hollow and smudged it around as if painting a dot on where he'd be.

"At around eleven, I'm going to put on a little drive ..."

He swept his beam to the left, further up Frigg's Hollow, then made a hooking-back motion with his arm, the light beam curling around.

" ... and circle through the edge of the Slashings ..."

He swung the flashlight around until it pointed ahead and to the left, again making the little circling motion.

" ... and will swing past Stef up in Big Buck Hollow."

JR and Stef nodded.

"All right boys. Let's go get 'em."

Stef locked his flashlight on the reflector up ahead and made a beeline toward it, placed head-high on an oak tree. He had to take a leak, which meant taking off his gloves and working through the layers of clothing. Once finished, he glanced back and saw the twin cones from their lights creeping away.

Shining his light forward was like peeking through a thick black curtain, a narrow and detached view of the forest. Up until this point, he had a good idea where they were, but just had to follow his old man's lead. Before the cat's-eye tacks had seemed bright as streetlights, but now that it was up to him to find the path they appeared their actual size, smaller than a dime, easy to miss in a sea of black ink.

He crept forward, scanning slowly left to right and back again in a narrow arc, knowing that his old man purposely set the tacks in a generally straight line, no sharp turns, else they would be too easy to miss. Each time a glimmer reflected back, a wave of stress released, only to have the anxiety build back up when sweeping for the next marker.

The ground rose as he ascended the side hill at the entrance of Big Buck Hollow, then leveled off again when he reached the bench, a flat strip about twenty yards wide that continued at this elevation up to the head of the hollow. It was easy to follow the trail here, as there were natural guardrails, to the right the sharp drop off into the hollow, to the left a side slope leading up to the summit of the hill.

He reached a cat's-eye placed in the remnant of a dead tree, standing like a plinth all alone, branches long gone, the bark stripped away, conk-shelf mushrooms jutting out like stair-steps in a spiral around the trunk, dots and gouges where insects and woodpeckers had pecked at the rotting wood.

Stef leaned a hand against it to catch his breath, and scanned beyond with the flashlight. The next marker twinkled. Not far now …

His reflexes made him jump backward before he even was conscious of the sound—something moving and tumbling. An alarm blazed in his head—*The old tree is falling!* —and he immediately scrambled backward, stumbled onto one knee, arms instinctively shooting up to cover his head, dropping the flashlight in the process but saving his rifle from slipping off his shoulder.

He knelt there, braced for a crash.

Nothing.

He retrieved the flashlight and shone it back at the dead tree, still standing intact. But at the base there was a scurrying sound and the light beam revealed a spiked ball rolling around on the ground near a hole in the tree.

A porcupine!

He must have woken it up. The sound was from it scrambling down the hollow inside of the dead tree. In the flashlight beam, its eyes reflected back at him just like the tacks. It shook itself awake, long quills ruffling, and then paced back and forth, as if bothered by all the fuss but not willing to leave its den.

Stef wasn't afraid of porcupines, the idea they could shoot quills was something used to frighten children. But he didn't want to make any noise to shoo it off either, afraid he'd also spook any deer in the vicinity.

From this angle, he was having trouble picking up the next cat's-eye, but he triangulated where he'd last seen it in relation to the dead tree and continued onward in that direction.

After twenty, thirty, forty yards he still hadn't found the next marker. Now he had entered a patch of beech, their pale curled leaves effectively forming a screen by catching the light beam, making it difficult if not impossible to see beyond.

It took effort to get to his wristwatch, having to tug back three layers of cuffs—his coat, the flannel, the thermal underwear—and at same time pry back the edge of the thick ski glove as well, opening his right finger and thumb like pincers to expose the watch dial. But he couldn't get the flashlight—in his left hand—to shine on the watch face, and couldn't press in the little illumination button on the side of the watch with his thick, gloved fingers. So he had to remove his right glove, biting the fingertips while he yanked his hand out, and repeat the pincer movement until he could feel the nub on the side. A faint green backlight revealed the liquid-crystal digits.

6:28 a.m.

He was supposed to be at his stand at 6:20. *Already eight minutes late!* And now he had lost the way in.

He shined the light behind, thinking maybe best to backtrack and start over from there, porcupine be damned ... but couldn't find the dead tree anymore among the other tree trunks. It would be worse to go backward and end up even more off course.

His mind raced. This was Big Buck Hollow—his old man's prized spot where his kid brother had gotten bucks the last two years in a row—offered to Stef this year out of the blue. *Why? Because of the acceptance letter?* More likely because of all the wood he chopped. Except he didn't chop it—Skate had! That was why they invited him to Finn's, why Doc gave him the knife, why Karl Thiassen offered him a job!

Such a fraud. And now he was going to botch the first day of the season by getting screwed up and not at his stand at first light—that first precious hour when the deer are moving because of all the hunters in the woods. That's when the chances were best to see action!

6:29 a.m. The clock was ticking. He'd already wasted a minute just standing there. *Like an idiot.*

He took a deep breath and tried to calm himself.

Even though he couldn't see it, he knew the top of Big Buck Hollow was shaped like a natural amphitheatre. The deer stand was like a skybox, high up, near the top rim, with a great vantage looking down into arena. No way a deer moving down here could see a hunter up along the hillside.

Marked trail or not, he had to be up there and settled in before the season started. Even if it wasn't the exact stand location his old man always used, as long as he had the right sight lines, able to see the head end where deer liked to cross, as well as an open look down into the draw, in case anything came up the hollow. *And without these damn beech trees blocking the view.*

He clicked off the flashlight and stood there in absolute darkness. He could hear the heavy droplets of water from the tree branches cascading onto the soft leaves of the forest floor. Gradually his eyes became adjusted to the gloom. Maybe he was imagining it, but the sky seemed one shade lighter than pure black—*the first sign of dawn?*—but enough that he could make out the shape of the encircling ridgeline.

He tucked his right glove into a front pocket and, hand bare, dug out his compass from inside his chest pocket, pressed the compass up to the lens of the flashlight, cupped his gloved left hand around it to shield his eyes, clicked the light on and purposely looked away, not wanting to kill his night vision. After a few seconds, he clicked the flashlight off. A phosphorescent dash and two dots glowed on the compass face—the dash was on the vibrating magnetic needle and the two dots marked zero degrees on the compass dial. The idea was to point the compass in the direction of travel, turn the compass dial until the dash lined up between the two dots, and determine the bearing.

He looked at the faint outline of the ridge, pictured his map, and lined up the compass. The stand would be north–northeast of his present position. He started to walk forward in the dark, one step at a time, one hand held out in front of him to shield himself from walking into low sapling branches that could poke his face or eyes. About every ten steps, he checked the compass to make sure he was still on course and hadn't drifted.

He sensed the gain in elevation, the slope increasing. The shapes of the tree trunks and branches were now visible against the sky, which helped with his sense of orientation but increased the urgency.

The shadow of the ridgeline was getting lower in his line of vision as he approached the top of the bowl.

He checked his watch again. 6:39 a.m.

It was time to find a place to stand and get settled in. He clicked on the flashlight and immediately his night vision retreated. He swept the light slowly in an arc, examining each individual tree. Was it big enough around that it would shield his profile when standing behind it, but not so big that to see around the other side would require a lot of movement? Was the ground near the base flat enough to stand on? There was nothing worse than having to stand for hours while leaning on an angle or having a root under the sole of a boot. He couldn't assess the vantage point in the dark, but would have to trust that just about anything up this high on the side hill would provide decent lines of sight. Lastly, he shone the light upward to make sure no widowmakers—broken branches—were dangling overhead.

He found one black cherry tree that met the criteria, and as a bonus there was a fallen tree trunk on the ground immediately behind it that he could sit down on.

It was unmistakable that the sky was lightening into charcoal gray, individual trees and branches visible in silhouette.

He scraped away the leaves and sticks around the base of the tree with his muck boots, then kicked at the ground, turning up some soft humus for him to stand and move around on. This made a racket but there was no way to avoid it, and once clear, he could move from side to side silently.

By this point, he was sweating profusely from the climb. It was tempting to unzip his coat completely and unbutton his shirt, but that was a quick way to lose all of the hard-won body heat.

He unshouldered his rifle and propped it on the ground, leaning up against the tree, checking a few times that the base was stable and it wouldn't tip over. It took a bit of contorting to twist around and extract his lunch from the rear pouch. He took a deep swig of the sports drink, stowed the apple in a front pocket, then resealed the lunch bag and tucked it under the log behind him for easy access.

He lifted the Mohawk and pulled back the bolt, opening the breech, then fished around in his front pocket and edged four bullets out of the clip with his thumbnail and palmed them. In order to have both hands free while he loaded the gun, he tucked the flashlight underneath his chin, squeezing it against the collar of his jacket—incredibly awkward—as moving his head at all would cause it to fall. He jammed the butt of the rifle into his armpit and held the stock in his left hand, his neck and side in agony as he used his free right hand to click each bullet into the magazine.

One-two-three-four. He slid the bolt forward, making sure the first round chambered smoothly.

He clicked off the flashlight and pocketed it, checked his watch one more time. 6:44 a.m. *With five minutes to spare!*

He wriggled his hand inside his glove, shouldered the rifle, and stood next to the tree on the scraped patch of earth. He ate the apple, one crisp, cold bite at a time. When he got down to the core, he rubbed the apple against the bark at head height. Supposedly it would help mask his scent. He doubted that actually worked, but it was a tradition his old man always did, and Stef did not want to screw up Big Buck Hollow any further.

He became aware of his coat—not actually orange yet—but the first color other than a variant of black that was visible. The low cloud cover from the earlier rain had begun to lift and a mottled halo appeared above the distant ridge of the Shawmut Grade to the southeast. The canopy of bare branches formed a complex web against the lightening sky, as if finely etched in ink.

The slope and contour of the terrain were emerging, individual features perceptible in shades of gray. In the dark it felt like he had covered a lot of distance, climbed a near-vertical slope, but now he could see the beech saplings were only fifty yards away, the dead tree less than a hundred, and the bank of the hillside was gradual, not the steep climb he had imagined.

The forest floor took on hues, mostly brown and tan with flecks of red, orange, and yellow, tufts of green ground pine here and there, green patches of moss on the sides of tree trunks and fallen logs. The clouds had some texture, still gray, but blotches of the palest pink shone through in places. It was the same drab November woods and sky as ever, but after the long walk in the dark, everything seemed projected in Technicolor.

And then there was a distinct moment where he could see all the details of the surrounding landscape fully in sharp relief.

It was daylight.

To his left was a natural saddle that defined the head-end of the hollow, an easy way for deer bedded down on the ridgetop to transit across to the Slashings or vice versa. The low point of the saddle was a wide-open shot about seventy-five yards away.

Directly in front of him the ground rolled down into a depression—the center of the bowl-shaped draw—populated by black cherry trees standing straight and tall and spaced evenly, with almost no ground cover to speak of. It was a near-perfect stretch of ground.

Beyond, a side-slope ascended to the opposite rim of the bowl where a row of pine trees stood. The view across was open enough for a long-range but unlikely shot.

To the right, the cluster of beech saplings obstructed a clear view around the dog-leg bend, meaning anything coming up from the bottom of the hollow would be screened from him until it was fifty yards away. He'd have to be alert in that sector.

Just a peek of the main valley of Frigg's Hollow was visible as a small triangle, down near the running brook, almost 300 yards away—way too far for any realistic shot, but possible to detect movement and, if it came up the draw, be ready.

Continuing right past the beech trees was the tapering end of the bench and the dead tree—the way he came in. It was possible that something could work up from there and be on top of him in a hurry.

Behind him, the hill tilted up another twenty yards to the ridgeline. He had to fully pivot his body around to look up there, it was essentially a blind spot. Unlikely anything would come from that direction, but if it did he would have to rely on hearing it coming before he could see it.

He had just completed the circuit with his eyes when the first shot boomed out in the distance. It came from over the far hilltop, in the general direction of Bear Behind but to the left and most likely all the way from Frey's Hollow, almost two miles to the south, where the Sauers crew hunted.

As he listened there was a second pop then, after a beat, a third.

That deer was running. *Must have missed on the initial shot.*

But it was much too far away to matter.

Stef cycled through the sectors again: the saddle ... the bowl ... the rim beyond ... the beech trees ... the triangle ... the bench ... the dead tree ... the side hill ... the ridgeline behind him.

Already the shapes and patterns were becoming familiar, disjointed, like pieces of a jigsaw puzzle to stare at and examine.

His senses played tricks.

Was that the shape of deer? A glance through the rifle's scope revealed it was nothing but a stump.

Was that a flicker of tail? No, a chickadee swooping from branch to branch.

That swoosh-swoosh-swoosh sound, that had to be deer moving through wet leaves. No, just a squirrel bounding across the forest floor.

That rustling sound, was that the scrape of a hoof? No, it was the beech leaves rattling in the breeze.

All the while he shifted his weight from foot to foot, held the rifle cross-body so it was ready to raise into shooting position at a moment's notice, then over his shoulder by its strap, easy to slip off quickly, then on the ground, propped against the tree, where he could easily reach and grab it.

The distant bang of a rifle. Someone, somewhere was getting lucky.

Above the treeline, low scudding clouds crossed the sky. The early light faded into a dull gloom, and with it his spirits. He hazarded a look at his watch. 8:05 a.m. The first hour already gone and no action but a stupid squirrel. And a porcupine.

By this time last year, his kid brother had bagged a nice six point.

Down in the triangle, two bright orange figures appeared, walking up from the bottom of Frigg's Hollow. At this distance, they moved silently and in slow motion, vanishing behind trees and reappearing, inching across the narrow slice of view. Just the way they walked, the same blaze orange-and-camo coats and hats they wore, he was certain they were the Sauer twins.

What were they doing up here in Frigg's Hollow?

They vanished from sight and for a panicked few minutes he pictured them turning left and coming up the draw of Big Buck Hollow, shielded from view by those damn beech trees.

But then at the farthest-out point he could see—where the main hollow continued past Big Buck—he glimpsed two orange dots, creeping away.

So they were going to hunt the head end of Frigg's Hollow. That would make for one long drag back to the lake. Though knowing those two, they'd happily carry a buck out on a pole over their shoulders. Or more likely, they'd ignore the posted signs and drive their ATV up there.

Then it struck him they would be located right below the Slashings. With his luck, when his old man put on a drive at eleven, he'd end up kicking deer right down to them...

He was so busy ruminating on the Sauer twins that it took a flicker of movement from his peripheral vision to grab his attention and snap him back to focus.

A deer!

Walking up the center of the draw into the middle of the bowl, already much closer than he would have expected, less than fifty yards away. He had been too preoccupied to notice it enter his field of vision, and that cost him precious seconds to get ready.

It was a small deer, with a short neck and square body, its winter coat gray-brown and well camouflaged against the drab forest background, traipsing along in no particular rush, ducking its nose down to nibble at something on the ground. A six-month-old fawn.

From time to time it turned to look behind, and Stef shifted his attention. Sure enough, there was a second deer.

Hanging back. Noticeably bigger.

This deer didn't move as lacksadically as the fawn, each step was measured and it looked around on high alert. Probably they bedded down on the far side, where there was bench overlooking Frigg's Hollow, and woke when Sauer twins moved through.

Was that a flash of antlers atop its head?

Stef very slowly stooped, grabbed the barrel of the propped-up Mohawk with his left hand, lifted it vertically inch by inch, as slowly as he could, until he could get his right hand on the stock at belt-level, trying to keep the whole motion hidden behind the tree trunk, all the while keeping his eye on the big deer and for any sign it was spooked.

He needed to get a scope on that deer to see if it had antlers.

But before he could raise the rifle up to his shoulder, the edge of his vision grabbed his attention again. While he had been fixated on the second deer, the fawn had continued meandering forward and now was really close to Stef, only about ten yards away. Any motion would immediately alert the fawn and, by extension, the other deer.

Stef stood there completely frozen, the rifle held awkwardly in front of him, pressed to his chest like he was sliding down a fire pole.

The fawn could sense something was there. This close, he could see its flopsy ears twitching, its black eyes and oversized lashes as it cocked its head side to side, trying to make him out. Deer were color-blind and couldn't see the blaze orange, but regardless he was a big patch of ... whatever colors deer saw ... lumped on to the side of the tree trunk.

The fawn stomped its front leg and flared its nostrils. *Was the apple actually working?*

Stef's neck and shoulders and arms were starting to burn from holding the rifle vertically. He felt his body start to shake from trying to stand so motionless, used every bit of mental power to will the deer to look away and move onward.

Which it did. The fawn didn't continue any further toward Stef, instead turned and headed up toward the saddle, but now at a trot, its bushy white tail swishing up once or twice. Stef immediately snapped his head around to relocate the bigger deer, which was starting to move as well.

It was now or never—Stef had to get the rifle up and into shooting position. Which he did.

Both deer were starting to hustle now. It took a second for Stef to relocate the trailing deer with his plain vision, calculate a little in front so when he looked into the scope he would be able to re-acquire it.

His first glance through the scope was disorienting, everything appearing in a yellow hue.

The scope covers!

Already the deer were getting up into the saddle and in a few seconds they would be gone. Stef flicked off the safety and slid a gloved finger up against the trigger. The moment he had an open shot he would have to fire.

The big deer paused after it ascended a little rise and for an instant stood in profile at the low point of the saddle.

This time Stef immediately found it in his scope, eyes anticipating and immediately adjusting to the optic yellow haze. The deer appeared much farther away than he expected. He had a nice clear shot at the shoulder ... but instead moved the crosshairs up and to the left to check the deer's head.

No antlers.

Another doe.

Stef let out a long exhale and the gun sagged.

He watched the two deer scamper up the curve of the saddle, not in the direction of the Slashings as he had expected, but instead up onto the ridgetop, above and behind him. A tangle of wild grapevines decorated the front of the hill up there, a good place to bed down again.

He sat down heavily on the log behind the stand, taking the strain off his knees. He rooted around in the lunch bag—this called for a candy bar. As he sat there munching, replaying the encounter in his mind's eye, the rain started up again.

At first it seemed like an extension of the showers earlier in the morning, a light even drizzle. But heavy raindrops started to plunk and splatter all around him. The tone of the sky abruptly shifted to an ominous charcoal.

Then it poured.

He fumbled around in his rear game pouch, found the orange plastic poncho, unfolded it from its container, and draped it over his body. He poked his head through the neck opening, pulled the plastic hood up over his hunting cap. He knew he looked ridiculous, like he was wearing an orange garbage bag, but there was no one to see him and it was better than getting completely soaked.

He pressed his body as close as he could to the tree trunk—as if it could somehow offer some shelter—and held the rifle pointed barrel-down, notched in a crooked elbow underneath the poncho to keep it dry.

The clouds lowered and appeared to brush the treetops, which swayed back and forth. The opposite hillside vanished behind a shimmering gray curtain. With his face pressed close to the black cherry tree, he watched rivulets form on the scaly bark and braid, then change course, saw the smeared chunks of apple from earlier.

The poncho offered only so much protection. Water seeped in around the neck hole. He couldn't hold the gun for long and propped it on the ground against the tree, making sure no little rivers funneled into the barrel, trying to keep it draped under an extended wing of his poncho, without much success.

He squinted up at the gray sky. A patch of sky was lightening to southwest. Maybe this was just a passing shower, quickly moving through.

But the rain only increased in intensity, falling so hard it made a crackling sound like bacon sizzling in a pan with the flame being turned up.

He tried to stand as still as he could, reducing his surface area. Every little motion caused more rain to seep through the poncho in new places, finding crevasses in his outer gear: the gap at his wrist between coat and glove, the inside of his collar, dripping down between his shoulder blades, the bunched-up wool pants at the top of his muck boots.

The temperature must have been hovering right at freezing. When he shifted because he couldn't hold still any longer, not only did a new cascade of leaks spring inside his clothing but thin sheets of ice crackled and slid off the poncho.

He became fixated, staring intensely at one spot—the dip in the saddle—and the rest of the rainswept landscape receded, almost like he was looking through a tunnel. He pictured the deer standing there, imagined it had antlers. He had a clear shot. Yes, he would still be caught in this rain storm—but he would be on the triumphant side of the equation, a sequence that would end with him back at camp sitting by a roaring fire.

His hands went numb. He tried to get inside his front cargo pockets, but the ski gloves were too thick, so he tugged them off, the cold, damp air and rain hitting his bare skin like an electric shock. He located the packet of handwarmers. His hands were too wet and cold to grasp and tear the plastic, so he used his teeth to rip the container open. The pouches were like little tea bags that he shook to catalyze the iron dust inside, generating heat as they oxidized. He slid the pouches inside his wet gloves and squirmed his freezing hands back inside. The interior of the gloves was still mostly dry, though a few tiny seams between his fingers were damp. He gripped the hand-warmer pouches as tightly as he could, trying to squeeze out every degree of warmth.

While this series of movements resulted in warmer hands, it all but eliminated the usefulness of the poncho and now he was wet everywhere.

The bill of his hunting cap had soaked through, droplets beaded on the edge and fell on his cheeks and nose, ran down his chin and neck. The light grew dimmer and dimmer and it seemed like daybreak in reverse.

He lost all track of time, but didn't want to execute the check-watch maneuver, which entailed a new range of motion and a new set of leaks.

He began to shake.

And then—just as suddenly as it started—the downpour stopped, as if someone had turned off a shower faucet.

At first, he couldn't believe it and just stood there numb, shivering, hugging the tree and bracing for the next torrent. But the sky in fact did lighten and jagged breaks appeared in the clouds. Behind the storm front, the air turned noticeably colder, the damp air now with a brisk bite to it.

Anything was better than that rain.

He removed the poncho, shook it clear of water and sheet ice, and tried to fold it back into a neat square, but ended up with something more like a loaf of orange plastic. Rather than try to fit the jumble back into his game pouch, he jammed it under the log next to the lunch bag.

He performed a bunch of leg squats, knowing how silly he looked, but they got his circulation going again. Then he pulled out the flask from his hip pocket and took a deep sip of blackberry wine. An amazing warmth spread down his throat into his chest. He took another long swig.

He checked his watch. The liquid crystal display was sluggish and it took a few seconds for faint digits to materialize: 88:88. The rain must have leaked in and zapped it. *What a stupid cheap watch!* His old man insisted on using mechanical watches, but Stef thought the digital watch looked cool when he asked his mom to buy it for him.

Well there was nothing much to do but wait for his old man to put on his mini-drive, not that he'd know when it commenced.

He was ravenous. Sitting on the seat cushion on the log, he unpacked the bagged lunch. Thankfully, it was still dry. The ham sandwich had been completely smooshed by now and was cold, but it tasted like the best ham sandwich ever. He chewed each bite slowly, tasting the salt of the ham, the sharp cheddar, creamy mayo, and tangy mustard, washed it down with the cherry sports drink, trying to stretch the moment out as long as he could.

But soon it was gone and there was nothing else to do but get back on stand. As he stood there, he munched on a bite-sized candy bar, semi-frozen from the falling temperature, chewy to the point he was afraid it might dislodge a filling from his teeth.

He worked through the visual circuit again and again, paying special attention to the saddle coming from the direction of the Slashings, as well as the opposite hillside. If his old man kicked anything out in front of him, most likely it would come that way.

The uniform gray cloud cover of earlier had parted and now was fully ripped asunder, exposing a mix of ragged dark and frosty white clouds, with shards of bright blue sky poking through in places, shafts of slanted sunlight lancing down and illuminating a patch of forest for a few seconds and then winking shut like a closing eye.

Time passed and Stef zoned out for a while.

To break the monotony, he walked a few yards to the side and took a leak. He scanned around as he did, not wanting this to be the moment a deer happened by. After, he scraped wet leaves over the spot to dampen down the scent.

The wind picked up, the tops of the trees swayed side to side, and branches clacked and clattered into each other. From high up came a roaring sound that sounded like a jet plane cruising above in a circle, now close, now far away.

On the opposite hilltop a little fleck of orange inched along the ridge line, disappeared for a while, then popped back into sight, growing in size, meandering through the trees, until finally emerging out of the thick cover and materializing into the shape of his old man.

Stef watched him cross the saddle onto this side of the hollow and make a beeline for a location about fifty yards to Stef's left, closer to the head-end. His old man looked puzzled. Stef realized he was concealed pretty well here, so stepped out and waved. His old man waved back and approached, rifle shouldered, taking a weaving path along the pitched side slope to get to Stef.

When he arrived he was clearly winded, clothes wet, cheeks flushed from the drive he'd put on, but in good spirits, undaunted by the weather or the hike through the Slashings.

"Any luck?" his old man asked.

"A couple doe came through, a little after eight." Stef pointed up at the ridge behind them. "Headed up there."

His old man took a moment to look around, at the saddle, down into the bowl, over at bench.

"This is a good spot," he said. "I like how you have more of a view down into the valley and the bench over there, but still have the head end covered. And a better view across."

"I got a little mixed up in the dark," Stef confessed.

"No, you did a good job. I think maybe this is better …"

Stef was floored to hear that.

"Except for those beech trees down there."

His old man asked Stef to get his lunch out of the rear pouch so he wouldn't have to twist around. He immediately gulped down the sports drink, opened up the ham sandwich, and looked at Stef.

"Already ate," Stef said. "After the rain moved through."

"That sure was something. Reminded me of the first day back in '81 …"

"Dad."

"Okay, okay. It was just a similar cloudburst is all …"

He thought about telling his old man about his watch, but didn't want to hear the standard lecture about cheap plastic overseas junk and buying American and his general philosophy of things: *Take good care of it and it will last you a long time.*

So they both were silent as his old man ate his sandwich.

"You see anything?" Stef asked after a while.

He spoke out of the side of his mouth while he chewed. "Nothing at Bear Behind. A few shots just after first light, behind me, over in Frey's Hollow."

"Running deer," Stef said and his old man nodded, mouth full.

After devouring the rest of the sandwich, he continued, "On the drive. I did see a couple of hunters up further—" he pointed "—up near the head end of Frigg's Hollow. So, I took a wider circle and that put me a little deeper into the Slashings than I wanted. It sure is easy to get mixed up in there. At one point I came out and was looking down into Naval Hollow…"

Naval Hollow was an entirely different valley and watershed that ran far to the northwest and ended at the lake where Straight Creek flowed in, easily five miles in the wrong direction.

"But I realized it right away. The sun coming out helped me see the hollow was going the wrong way. So, I cut a course back here. And deep in the middle of the Slashings, something moved out ahead of me. Two deer …"

"Maybe the ones that came by here? One was a fawn."

"No, these were both big deer. They didn't spook or anything. Kept their distance from me. Just out of sight, couldn't get a real look. Then they vanished."

They both stood in silence for a while, his old man contemplating what the next move was. Stef was getting antsy, ready for anything to break up the monotony, get his blood flowing.

"This wind isn't good," his old man observed. "We're going to have to keep trying to move them."

"I could head up to the ridgetop and push across the flat up there, through the grapevines, over the summit," Stef suggested. "Maybe send something over to JR or the General, or kick something down here to you."

His old man instantly agreed. "That's a good idea."

Then added, "—but I'll put on the drive. You stay here. This is too good a spot."

Stef was about to protest, but saw the set in his old man's jaw.

"Okay," Stef replied.

His old man shouldered his rifle. "I will cross the flats on top of the hill and circle over to the General. A half hour. If nothing moves, go pick up your brother at Blind Man's and then we'll all meet up at Headquarters. Make a plan for the afternoon."

Stef nodded, resigned to it. *A half hour wasn't that bad in the big scheme.*

His old man retraced his path back up to the head-end of the hollow and crossed the low point of the saddle, but this time he continued forward and up into a little notch in the ridgeline and disappeared.

Stef was too drained to stand any longer and sat down on top of the log, propped the rifle across his knees, his body oriented toward the saddle so he could see the ridgetop above him by looking left. Given the path his old man was travelling, it was theoretical something could come over the front edge heading toward the bench, a natural path of escape.

He idly watched as the clouds were swept from the sky, racing past like they were in a hurry to get somewhere, exposing brilliant blue skies beyond. Light and shadow alternated like a slow strobe in the draw—one moment dark and gray, the next brightly lit, the trees casting long shadows.

The wind was picking up and gusting, causing the leaves on the beech trees to vibrate and rattle incessantly. Creaks and groans from the swaying trees made him imagine he was seated in the crow's nest of a tall ship at sea ... the trees as masts ... the hillsides giant waves cresting ... off on an expedition to explore the Artic.

KA-BOOOOM!!

He was snapped out of his daydream by a booming rifle shot, coming from the hilltop right above him.

His whole body flinched reflexively and he immediately was standing, holding the rifle crosswise at his chest, without even realizing it.

His old man. *He must have kicked out a buck.*

Stef scanned the ridgeline and the saddle, tense, ready—something might run past at any moment.

The seconds stretched into minutes. The wind continued to gust and swirl. The initial rush of adrenaline began to fade.

Then came the shrill unmistakable sound of a whistle blowing. One … two … three … and finally, a fourth whistle.

His old man got a buck!

And then the next thought hit like a hammer: *On the drive I was supposed to make.*

He was in motion before he even thought about it, walking up toward the head end, following the course his old man had taken. He had his rifle at the ready because who knew. Only when he reached the saddle did he realize he'd left the lunch bag and his poncho behind at the stand.

As he was looking back, he noticed fresh deer droppings near his boots, deer tracks in the mud and scattered leaves. The big doe from this morning was standing right here when he scoped it. Back at his stand he could see the rolled up orange poncho under the log and pictured himself standing there, rifle raised, finger on the trigger.

There was another series of four whistles, blaring like a summons, and Stef continued onward, leaving his stuff behind for now.

At the end of the draw, he cut through the little notch that acted like a natural path up to the top of the hill, relatively flat with a small slant to the north leading up to the summit. The wind was noticeably stronger up here, giant trees swaying fluidly, which was disconcerting. Thick ropes of wild grape vines hung from the trees like tangled knots of hair caught in a giant's comb.

He couldn't spot his old man anywhere, so dug out his whistle from inside his coat and blew one solid blast. After a few seconds, he received two whistles in response, coming from just over the summit of the hill.

He ascended the gradual slope and when he reached the crest—a sort of rounded knuckle of ground—there stood his old man and kid brother. JR must have run the whole way over here when he heard the four whistles.

As he approached, he saw they were standing alongside the body. The buck was lying on its side with legs sprawled out as if in mid-leap, a grayish coat with a white underbelly, its head and thick neck lolled off to the side, purple tongue sticking out of side of its mouth comically. Stef counted six points in total, a Y forward and a vertical tine near the base, with a good wide spread. Long, fine lashes sprouted around its big glassy eyes, open and staring up at nothing.

Little mites crawled in and out of the hair around its nose. There was a little tuft of fur behind its front shoulder with a red eye at the center where the bullet had entered.

"Nice deer," Stef said flatly.

"Thank you," his old man replied.

Stef could tell from the way his old man was looking at him that he was being read like an open book.

"When I came up through the grape vines, two deer that were bedded down jumped up and dashed off. One of them a fawn like you said. I froze. They didn't run far though—about twenty-five yards— and then stopped, milled around. The big doe was looking up here at the summit. I turned and there he stood right near the crest. I could see the horns clearly against the sky. Didn't wait another second, pulled up and fired. It went right down."

"Wow," Stef said. "Pretty good timing." He almost had to spit out the words through clenched teeth.

JR was looking back and forth between them, puzzled as to what was going on.

"Here's the thing. There was another deer. Standing behind the one I shot. I only noticed it when the deer went down. It didn't run at the sound of the rifle shot, just stood there a moment, looking at this buck fall, looking at me. Then it turned and bounded off that way—" he pointed towards the Slashings, the edge of which was visible two hundred yards to the right across the flat like a thick scribbled line.

"It was an enormous deer, Stef. Easily ten points."

"You're kidding."

His old man shook his head in a way that meant he was not.

A shrill whistle sounded off to their left, in the direction of Spike Point. JR gleefully blasted out two whistles in reply, and a few minutes later a hunter with an orange coat and red hat appeared. The three of them stood watching the General approach, picking a path up the gradual slope toward them.

His old man turned to him and said, "I really wish it was you, Stef."

Stef avoided looking at the buck and said nothing.

When the General arrived, he took a moment examining the deer and said. "Nice shot, Jack."

His old man eagerly repeated the story, adding a little embellishment that made it sound like he'd felled the buck on the run with a hip shot.

"So there's another buck," the General said after the story finished.

This whole time Stef had stood to the side, looking off into the distance, as if he'd climbed up here to take in the view. And the view from the knob was spectacular, stretching for miles in every direction. To the east and south the purple line of the Shawmut Grade under cold blue skies, the dark shadowy fist of Hel's Hill rising to the west, and to the north, the high, rolling plateau.

Stef blinked. Towering above the line of the horizon to the northwest rose a solid bank of pure white that looked like a wall, the front edge billowing out.

The General was in the middle of saying something when Stef interrupted—bringing unexpected sharp looks from both the General and his old man. Nobody interrupted the General.

"Look at that cloud," Stef said, pointing.

They all turned and looked up, because in just the few moments since Stef had spotted it the cloud had grown in size and proximity and now appeared to be a vertical cliff rising nearly straight up above them.

"Lake effect," his old man said.

And as he said it, wispy snowflakes started dancing around them like fluttering moths.

"Here's the plan," the General announced, in the voice he used to issue commands. "Jack, you stay here with the deer. JR, you go back to Blind Man's. Stef, head down to Big Buck. I am going to go into the Slashings and move that buck out." He said it as a statement of fact.

"Jack, if it comes back through here, don't hesitate. We'll figure out the tag later."

His old man nodded.

"I will circle around and meet up with Stef. If no action, we will meet back here. JR, we will whistle for you. Come right away."

"I will!" JR exclaimed.

"Okay, men. We don't have much time with the weather moving in. So let's go."

And without waiting, the General spun on his heels and marched off toward the Slashings.

"You heard him," his old man said.

Stef walked back down the slope, retracing the path he took to get here, moving with urgency. He felt his heart pumping, the blood moving through his limbs.

At the same time, the maneuver the General described had a pretty slim chance of actually working. Even assuming the buck was still in there, the Slashings were impossibly dense. You could be twenty yards from a deer and not even see it.

He descended into Big Buck Hollow. Out ahead of him to the south the skies were still clear blue, the sun glinting like a diamond, but directly above was like a cresting wave of smoke. Snow was swirling all around, like walking through a snow globe. He saw the splotch of orange poncho that marked his spot and hurried over.

He got back to his stand just as the snow began in earnest, the wind blowing with little particles of sleet mixed in. The wall of cloud passed overhead and closed down the blue sky. The gleaming sun was reduced to a small pale disk and it grew dark.

Now the storm swept into the hollow in full force, the wind howling as if unchained and let loose. Trees flexed and groaned, the sleet came sideways like needles against his cheeks. He tugged up the balaclava scarf until it was above his nose, leaving just a narrow strip for his eyes to peer out.

Giant shimmering curtains of snow rushed down the hollow, removing visibility in a series of waves: first the bottom of the hollow vanished, then the midpoint where the dead tree stood, then it was all around him, whooshing in and out, swirling like dervishes. *A whiteout.*

He hunkered as tightly as he could, thinking it would blow through, but the storm only increased in fury, the wind shrieking through the trees as limbs creaked and snapped.

Without warning, there was a bright flash and a moment later a loud crack followed by a rolling, booming rumble. At first he thought it was a tree falling, but then realized what it was.

Thunder snow!

He was terrified to look up … then finally did look up … and was bewildered by what he saw, the blizzard rushing past overhead like a raging river in the sky.

Out of the corner of his eye, flashing in and out of the sheets of snow, a figure was moving. Moving against the tide of the driving wind. Moving toward him.

At first, he saw the tall figure of the General, leaning forward into the wind, having completed his circle maneuver and now coming over to ride out the storm alongside Stef.

But then the figure shifted and Stef's heart stopped. It was moving on four legs. Head and massive neck bent down close to the ground. The curve of antlers sweeping off to either side: a huge rack.

There was no time!

The rifle was already collecting snow in every crevice and in the bore. He lifted the gun up slowly, shaking it once to clear the snow. The gale-force wind, the swirling storm, seemed to recede to white background noise. He could hear the sound of his blood pounding as he willed the deer to not move and finally—after what felt like an eternity—the butt of the rifle was in his shoulder and he could look through the scope.

A fog of yellow. *The damn scope covers!*

Holding the gun pressed against his shoulder, with one arm he carefully reached up, felt the round plastic of the front scope cover, stretched the elastic forward so the cover was past the lip of the scope, and then let the elastic contract and the lightweight covers got swept aside and fell somewhere.

The maneuver felt like it was taking minutes, his shoulder screaming with fatigue by the time he got his left arm back underneath the stock to support the weight of the rifle.

The buck had continued forward, but was still there in front of him.

He looked through the scope. *Nothing but white!*

But then his eyes adjusted to the depth and he saw the shape, more of a flickering impression than a clear view, the curve of shoulder, the flat line of back.

He clicked the safety off, moved the crosshairs forward, locating the hunched shoulder which was starting to move, in motion now, moving forward—

Stef pulled the trigger.

He didn't hear the shot or feel the kick of the rifle, only a numb ringing in his ears that quickly was replaced by the roar of the wind as he snapped out of the trance.

The buck noticeably flinched, took a step sideways, swayed for a moment, then gathered itself, got its legs back, turned and bounded away into the storm.

Stef cursed, quickly ejected the shell, slammed another into the chamber, and shouldered the rifle again, but in that brief instant the buck was gone.

He tried to fix in his mind where it had been standing, not easy with the driving snow obscuring the landmarks. The center of the draw, just below the saddle, less than fifty yards away, maybe even closer. Holding the rifle at chest height, ready in case it was nearby and jumped up, he covered the ground, not taking his eyes off the spot for fear he'd lose it, even though it meant the snow was pelting him directly in the face.

When he reached the place he moved slowly, scanning the ground, concentrating. The wet leaves on the ground had flash-frozen and crinkled as he slowly swept his boot back and forth, scanning. The snow was starting to accumulate, filling in the low spots between the leaves.

He saw a bright red splatter. *Blood!*

He knelt down to examine and saw a little piece of pink lung tissue among the blood. Deer tracks in the mud were visible, starting to fill in with snow, but he could clearly see the skid where the buck had pivoted and bounded away.

Nearby a sapling bent sideways, shredded at about the height of his elbow, where the bullet must have sliced through right before striking the deer.

His mind raced as he tried to remember the protocol. With a lung shot, there was a chance the buck had just gone a short distance and dropped dead. Though finding it in this blizzard wasn't going to be easy.

It was also possible the buck would go and lie down, and if so, best to wait twenty minutes, a half hour as it bled out, dying outright or becoming too weak to run. If he chased after it now, possibly with a last burst of adrenaline the buck could sprint away and he would lose it completely.

And maybe the wound wasn't too serious, in which case they'd have to trail it. Though with that piece of lung, he felt of the three outcomes that was the least likely.

But in any of the scenarios, he would need help.

The raw fury of the storm had dropped in intensity the past few minutes, the gale-force wind had blown through and it actually was quieting down a bit, while at the same time the rate of snow was increasing. The sun was completely gone and everything had a soft bluish hue.

He wasn't even sure the sound of the whistle would carry, but had to try. He blew three sharp blasts. Counted to thirty and blew three more.

Then, as he waited, he tried to picture the full sequence of events.

Just given the size of its rack—easily a ten point. *Possibly twelve!* And with that thick neck, the buck had to be four, maybe even five years old. It was traveling with another buck, a younger six point. While bucks usually split up during the rut, that had ended a few weeks ago and during the winter it was pretty common for them to hang out in bachelor groups.

Maybe the old buck saw or heard or smelled hunters coming into the woods at dawn, remembered previous buck seasons, and headed right to safety, into the Slashings.

His old man put on his mini-drive at eleven, pushed the two of them ahead and out of the Slashings, and they had gone up to the summit of the hill, bedding down at the knob.

Then his old man put on the second drive at … noon? And bumped into the fawn and the big doe, lying down among the grapevines. That in turn caused the two bucks up at the summit to stand up, and his old man shot the six point. The old buck ran back into the Slashings.

Next the General went into the Slashings right before the snow hit, and must have pushed it out again. It came down into this hollow, probably down through the low point of the saddle, which Stef couldn't see in the whiteout. He spotted it out here in the middle, likely headed over toward the bench, maybe to hide out there. The bench provided a number of easy exits for a wily old buck if anything approached.

But when Stef shot it, it had reversed course and moved in the direction of the opposite rim. Back toward the Slashings.

Or possibly the buck just stayed at this elevation, not wanting—or able—to climb the opposite slope, followed this contour, and exited out the far side of the draw, up toward the head end of Frigg's Hollow.

Where the Sauer twins were hunting.

A faint warbling whistle snapped him out of his reverie. *Someone had heard him!*

He yanked out the lanyard from inside his coat and blew two whistles in response. Now he knew why they used plastic whistles. A metal whistle would have frozen to his lips.

A minute later, another single whistle, this time closer and with more confidence. It was coming from over near the dead tree, the bench, around the front of the hill. Which puzzled him, he didn't expect anyone coming from that direction.

After a few more calls and responses, an orange coat and hat appeared in the falling snow, heading his way rapidly. His kid brother. Stef waved him over.

"I heard a gun shot. Then three whistles," JR said breathlessly as he arrived. "Are you okay?"

"Yes. Just when the storm arrived, a monster buck came down through here and I shot it."

JR looked around, expecting to see a body lying nearby.

"No. I mean I hit it. I don't know if it's out there dead or lying down"

"During the blizzard?" JR asked. "I couldn't see a thing …"

Stef pointed to the ground to show JR the blood, but there was nothing there but snow.

"It was right here. The snow must have covered it up."

He kicked at the spot with his boot, expecting to reveal chunks of blood-stained snow. But it was all white.

Stef next went over to the snapped sapling.

"The bullet hit here, and then hit the buck."

Now his kid brother was looking at him with those moon eyes of his.

"Maybe we should go get Dad," JR said.

The snow was coming down even heavier than before.

"Look," Stef said, an edge to his voice. "I hit the buck. I'm going after it. You can go run back to Dad and tell him."

"Stef, I just think—"

"Go. I've wasted enough time with you already."

Stef marched off in the direction the buck had traveled. He half-expected his kid brother to be there at his heels, following along behind him. But when he turned back, JR was gone, headed up toward the head end of the hollow to get their old man. He quickly lost sight of him in the swirling snow.

So he was on his own. *Fine.*

He refocused his attention on the task at hand, picking up the trail. He walked in a slow zig-zag pattern, fanning outward, desperately looking for something, anything. It quickly became apparent this was going to be impossible. An inch of snow had already fallen, covering up any hoof prints or blood, with no sign of let up.

He crossed the main depression at the center of the bowl, where runoff from the rain had collected and formed a small shallow pond that was freezing over, snowflakes beginning to stick on the black glassy membrane of ice. Ahead of him, the hillside sloped upward toward the Slashings, and to the right the draw descended to a lower level and then ducked left around the point, rejoining the main valley of Frigg's Hollow.

He had a choice to make.

His heart told him to continue right, to get to the buck before it happened past the Sauer twins. Hunting etiquette was pretty clearcut on this point: *Finders keepers.* If they took the shot that brought the buck down, it was theirs. No matter if Stef had wounded it, slowed it down. They would say Stef had his chance. If he were a better shot the buck would already be his. And no hunter would disagree with them.

But his head told him that old buck would try to sneak back into the Slashings. Sure, it had been bounced out of there twice already today, but a deer its age would have experience, would sense how hard pursuit would be in that tangle of briars and saplings. Particularly when wounded, it would want to be on familiar ground.

So Stef started to climb up the hill face in front of him. This side was a steeper slope than the other side where his stand was, and with the snow, he slipped to his knees a couple times while scrambling upward. About halfway up the slope, he heard a loud snort coming from above, a sort of whistling-whoosh exhalation.

The buck was up there on the ridge!

The buck had likely snorted because it picked up Stef's scent or heard him slip.

He fought the urge to just run up the final twenty yards so he could see for sure. What was he going to do, tackle the deer and stab it to death? No, this was going to be a tricky approach.

He unshouldered the rifle and held it up near his shoulder—an awkward way to walk, especially while climbing a bank—but he knew that he'd have to be ready to shoot instantly if he came across the buck. He did a quick trial, picking out a spot on a tree up near the ridgeline and raising the rifle to see how fast he could get the crosshairs on it.

Once again, he saw a blank field of white when he looked through the scope. *The scope covers!* He had dropped them back at his stand and in the excitement had completely forgotten.

He lowered the rifle and peered into the front of the scope. Snow had fallen into the open cup of the lens while he was carrying it on his shoulder and had crystallized into a crusty layer of ice. There was no way to chip it off without jostling the scope and running the risk it was no longer zeroed in, plus no way to keep it from icing up again. He could have slipped the plastic lunch bag over the scope, or wadded up the paper towel, or cut a section of poncho, but all those were back at the stand too.

He didn't have time to cross the valley and back and, to be honest, with all the snow, wasn't sure even if he did, that he'd be able to find the exact tree where he had stood.

But the gun wasn't usable in its current state.

A desperate idea struck.

He plopped down seated on the bank. The seat cushion attached to his belt kept his butt dry, but because it was a slippery, plastic-coated disk he had to jam the heels of his muck boots into the ground to avoid tobogganing down the hill. He laid the rifle across his knees and took out the hunting knife Doc had given him.

The scope had two slotted screws at the base of the ring clamp that attached the whole unit to fixed rail mounts on the top of the rifle. He laid the sharp point of the knife into the groove and levered it counter-clockwise, as carefully as he could, knowing bad things could happen if the knife slipped. He kept his thick ski gloves on just in case.

It took some elbow grease, but the screw head turned. Very carefully, he spiraled the first screw free, then repeated the same on the second mount. He tucked the screws in the breast pocket of his coat, knowing there would be hell to pay if he lost them.

Then he detached the scope from the rifle.

The gun looked slim and naked without it, felt lighter. There was a beaded sight at the end of the barrel—he'd never shot an open-sighted rifle before—but he figured it couldn't be much different than shooting at small game with a shotgun. And with this weather, long-range shooting was out of the question. The snub-nosed Mohawk seemed perfect for close quarters in the Slashings.

He stowed the scope in his empty rear game pouch, conscious that precious minutes had been lost. He scaled the final pitch of the hill up to the ridgeline, the rifle help up at his shoulder, ready to shoot like the hero in a military movie who was raiding an enemy hideout. Foot by foot he got close to the top lip, and then he could see over it.

He half expected the buck to be sitting there looking at him, but there was nothing.

He took a few strides forward and saw a big oval pressed into the snow with a splotches of blood smeared around inside. This is where the buck had bedded down. And it was most definitely wounded.

He wished that JR was here to see.

He noticed bits of hair in the snow … flecks of pink tissue and froth … a set of tracks leading away—

His eyes caught a flash of motion up ahead—a tail flickering. Before he could even react, a dark shadow bounded into the Slashings.

Stef set off in pursuit.

A clear boundary marked where the old-growth forest gave way to the unchecked new growth that had sprung up in the past decade since the top of this hill had been clear-cut. Maples and beech trees rose to a level height of about twenty feet, growing in tight bunches, each in a competition to grow the tallest, grab sunlight, crowd out the neighboring trees, and become the towering old survivors decades from now.

The tracks stood out in the fresh snow, which now lay several inches deep. Swooshes from the buck's legs skimming the surface connected the dots from one hoof print to the next. Every ten yards or so was another smattering of blood, the only color in the landscape other than his orange hat and coat.

While finding the buck's path was easy enough, following the trail itself was a challenge. Underneath the main growth of trees was a second layer of younger saplings, even more compact, presenting whip-like branches at eye-level that required constant vigilance to avoid being scratched, especially with his focus down on the trail.

During the clear-cut, loggers had bulldozed stumps and deadfall into mounds that had since transformed into unpassable hedgerows, bristling with blackberry briars that ripped at clothes and exposed skin. The only way through was to go around. And each time he did, there was a moment where he thought he'd lost the path, and had to zig-zag until he picked up the tracks again, saw a splash of bright red.

Deep gouges left behind by the heavy machinery were now puddles filled with muck, which had iced over and were hidden underneath the snow. He had to jump backward to avoid going in to his knees.

This part of the hill was at the same elevation as the Shawmut Grade, pressed up into the underbelly of the clouds like a wire brush into wool. With the falling snow, everything was hushed. The intense concentration made everything else recede and it felt as if he were in an enclosed chamber.

With all the climbing and ducking and weaving, he was sweating hard and unzipped his jacket to avoid overheating. Every now and then, he caught a glimpse of a figure moving out ahead of him, but by the time he got his rifle up it had shifted just out of range behind a screen of trees.

There were a few solitary hemlocks left standing that normally could serve as landmarks, but with the snowfall, their crowns weren't visible above the roof of young trees. He wasn't really sure how far in he'd gone.

He came across another pair of boot tracks mostly filled in with snow and wondered, *Was it the General?* No, he had entered the Slashings before the storm. Then it struck him. *These were my tracks!* The buck had made a full circle. Amazing how quickly the heavy snow was erasing their mutual paths.

After circling around yet another tangled deadfall, he suddenly emerged from the Slashings into the regular forest once again.

He was looking down into the head end of a hollow, with a U-shaped saddle bridge and a bowl-shaped depression beyond. For a moment, he thought he had come full circle back to Big Buck Hollow.

But unlike Big Buck, in the center a wide spring welled up, wet rocks darkly visible underneath loafs of snow. The spring quickly became a rushing stream that tumbled down the embankment into a larger hollow beyond.

Stef had never hunted this far up Frigg's Hollow before, but the terrain matched the map he'd drawn to a T—of course, relying on the USGS quad map as a reference to fill in the places he hadn't actually ever been.

Now with the more open forest and snowy sidehills as backdrop, there was a good chance he'd be able to spot the buck from a greater distance and be able to get a shot off.

It also provided a sense of urgency, because if the Sauer twins were still hunting up here, the buck was headed right toward them.

The buck's tracks descended directly toward the spring. It was probably thirsty, he figured. Stef realized he was completely parched, too.

He pictured the sports drink left behind in the lunch bag under the log, could almost taste it. The dark gurgling water looked so tempting. He wasn't sure how water coming straight out of the ground would make him sick—there probably wasn't fresher water to be found anywhere—but he resisted the urge.

Instead he took out the hip flask and gulped down the rest of the blackberry wine. It didn't have the effect he'd hoped—he was still as thirsty as before—and now his stomach turned in a fiery knot.

Oh, well. Plenty of cold beer tonight back at camp.

He wandered the perimeter of the spring. He had become pretty accustomed to following the trail—it was so hard to miss in the fresh snow—that it took him a minute to realize that the tracks had vanished.

He fanned out in wider and wider concentric circles. No tracks, other than the increasingly frantic churn of his boots muddying the fresh snow.

After about ten minutes, he was desperate. *How was this possible?*

Where the braids of the spring coalesced into a single stream, a log had fallen across from one bank to the other, forming a bar about waist high, with deep cake of snow on top. And in the center of the log was a half-moon shape where the snow had been brushed away. And in that indent, there was a smear of blood.

The buck was walking in the stream!

Stef followed, levering himself over the fallen log, and walked splashing down the center of the stream in his muck boots. He scrutinized the snow banks on either side to see if the buck had exited the watercourse. At regular intervals, there were other fallen logs across the stream and, sure enough, on each one he saw a scrape of snow, a fleck of blood.

The channel of the stream grew wider, the side banks grew taller, and runoff from the earlier rain channeled in from side rivulets along the way, forming icicle falls and squeezing curlicue ice rings from exposed banks. Soon the stream was becoming difficult to walk in.

He climbed up to the top of the right-hand bank—the side of the hollow they hunted—and continued following the creek downstream, moving as slowly as he could, stopping to examine every possible sign, spending twice as long looking across to the other bank for tracks.

That line of prints, the buck? No, the tiny paws of a squirrel hopping.

That sequence of ruffled-up snow? No, a flop of snow that fell from an overhanging branch.

Was it even possible the buck could have stayed in the stream this long? He had doubts—the stream was now rushing past in force. He wondered if he should retrace his path, double-check the banks. Maybe he missed the exit point. *Was it possible the falling snow had already filled in the tracks?*

Then he saw a set of prints climbing up the opposite bank, clear as a highway, unmistakable red dashes marking the way. He could imagine the buck laboring to climb up that short slope.

Stef sensed he was close.

And as if in sync with his mood, the snow began to taper off, from the constant heavy flakes of earlier down into a fine, wispy haze. It could have been his imagination, but the sky overhead seemed to be lightening, the cloud lifting.

He worked his way down the bank to the stream. The water rushed past, black as oil. He tentatively put one of his muck boots in and was relieved to find it was only running a foot deep, midway to his calf, well within the range the boots could handle. The stream was no more than ten feet wide, just a few strides across.

Just before he reached the other bank, his boot slipped into a cavity beneath a creek rock. He stumbled and, as he tried to regain his balance, the current was enough to shift his foot sideways and cause him to fall forward. His left hand shot out to brace himself and jammed into the bank, his right hand clutched the rifle strap so it wouldn't fall off, and his knee dipped underwater.

Out of pure reflex, he cursed loudly and immediately clamberred ashore. But not fast enough. Icy water had soaked through his wool pants around the knee and into his left boot. His left glove was soaking wet, too, and full of mud and snow. He realized his seat cushion had become unclipped and had floated downstream.

He found a fallen log, brushed off the deep snow, and sat down. He jammed the wet glove into his rear game pouch along with the detached scope, to get it out of the way. The water created suction inside his boot, requiring considerable effort to tug it off. Once he yanked it free, he shook it a few times to get any free water out and propped the boot carefully in the snow so it wouldn't tip.

He removed the thick woolen sock, peeled off the nylon under-sock, and sitting there—with his bare foot raised ridiculously off the ground—he wrung out the water from both. Just the short exposure to the air and his foot was screaming from the cold.

He took out the second pair of handwarmers, ripped the plastic with his teeth, and shook them to activate. One of the pouches he pressed to the arch of his bare foot and pulled the damp stocking sock over the top, which did a good job of holding it place. Then he pulled the soggy wool sock on over that and slid his foot back into the muck boot.

He stood up tentatively. His feet still felt cold and wet, there was an awkward lump when he stood, but there was a faint trace of heat beneath his toes as well.

Next came the thin cotton shooting gloves, one went on his left hand, with the hand-warming pouch slipped inside against his palm. The handwarmer from the morning in his right glove was spent, and he put that in his rear game pouch as well. He was creating quite the collection back there.

He glanced at the orange seat cushion, stuck against a branch, bobbing up and down in the current in the center of the stream. *Another casualty.* No way was he wading back in for that.

He rejoined the trail. The buck had meandered along the left bank of stream for a while and Stef could see why—from this point forward the water plummeted down in a series of cascades. There was more blood, and more frequently now than before, with frothy pink bubbles.

Less than a hundred yards from where he slipped in the stream, the tracks showed the buck had stopped and turned around to look back. A pile of still steaming droppings marked the spot.

And then the buck had bolted. Bounding tracks shot straight up the steep hillside to a ridgeline topped by pine trees, looming high above.

He must have spooked the buck when he cursed.

He glanced back upstream to where he was. *So close!*

Stef looked up at the heights in dismay. Somehow, the buck had found another reservoir of adrenaline to get up there. Maybe its heart burst when it reached the top. Or … maybe the wound wasn't as serious as he thought and the buck was still fresh, in which case it would just keep running away again and again every time he got close.

Either way, he was going to need help. No way he could get to a deer up there alone—there needed to be at least one other hunter, to approach from both sides, cover the escape routes. And even if it were lying there dead up on the summit, he'd need help dragging it out.

And with this realization, it was like a spell was broken.

He'd been so focused on the chase, he had not given any thought to his kid brother, his old man, the General, Mac. He just pictured wowing them with a trophy buck. Now he wondered what they were doing. *Probably looking for me!*

He was on the wrong side of the stream, on the opposite side of the valley from where they hunted, and leery of crossing back over.

But he could continue down Frigg's Hollow until he was below Bear Behind, and blow his whistle. Then they could rally and come up with a plan to get this buck together.

Probably what I should have done in the first place, he thought sheepishly. But he was so certain he'd bring down the buck on his own, unassisted. Legendary. That would have been the kind of story his old man would tell for years to come: *Stef and the Big Storm.*

Knowing his old man, they would come across the Sauer twins and enlist their help.

Dejected, he started the long walk down the hollow, trudging through the deep snow. A wave of pure exhaustion threatened to sweep over him, but he pressed on. His mouth watered at the thought of those candy bars back in the lunch bag.

As he came around a bend, he stopped dead in his tracks.

To his left, another roaring stream cascaded down a jumble of rocks and joined the main stream he had been following, doubling the flow. This was a different hollow to the left, with even steeper inclines on each side, almost like a narrow canyon. Where the streams converged, the steep hills formed a needle-like point, and there was a dense copse of hemlock trees alongside the banks at the intersection.

Looking ahead, instead of broadening out into a wide U the way Frigg's Hollow did in the middle and lower sections, the valley remained a sharp V, and hooked off to the right out of sight.

This was not Frigg's Hollow.

His heart started to drum and his mind raced. *Where am I?*

He tried to picture the map, where he had been. From Big Buck Hollow, he had entered the Slashings, circled around, and come out … not to Frigg's Hollow. Could he have done the same thing his old man did, and come out in Naval Hollow? No, that was a dry hollow, no streams running through it, even with the rain. Not like these.

The Fortress.

He had gone further back in the Slashings, much further than he thought, and had come out on the north tine of the three hollows that made up the turkey foot. And this new hollow coming in at the waterfalls, that was the center branch.

That meant he was miles away from … anyone. It would be a five-mile hike down South Fork to get back to where the boat was docked or the Sauer's ATVs. And if he backtracked, climbed back up the north hollow of the Fortress, cut through the Slashings—*without getting mixed up!* —and came down Frigg's Hollow, that circuitous path was twice as hard, and also five miles. He'd walked a few hundred yards in the deep snow and already was feeling exhausted.

What time was it? If only that damn cheap digital watch didn't die on him …

As if reading his mind, when he looked up there was a weird rose coloring in the clouds. In the notched V of the valley to the southwest, the clouds were breaking and there was an orange glow in the sky.

The sun was setting!

No no no, he thought. *That can't be right ...*

The sun set at quarter to five this time of year. If his old man got his buck at say, 12:30, and the storm was at 1:30, maybe he shot the deer at ... quarter to two? He replayed waiting for JR, removing the scope, the grueling journey through the Slashings, losing the path at the spring, following along the stream one step at a time, slipping and having to wring out his socks.

Yeah, that easily was three hours.

Goddammit, how could I be so stupid? He was so fixated on the buck that all other thoughts were chased from his head.

Now the sky was a blaze of orange and for one brief instant he saw a flash of the sun before it slipped beneath the horizon. Already the canyon hollow to his left was draped in dark shadow, the snow was taking on a soft, purplish hue. One thing he knew about these hollows. Once the sun set, it got dark, fast.

He remembered the spring behind Thunderbird. That was not far from here, at least on his sketched map. But the more he thought about it—he would have to somehow cross this rushing stream, find the next valley—the third, southern toe of the turkey foot—then ascend it in the dark. And how would he determine which of the many feeder streams flowing in was the one that led up to the spring by the cabin? Plus the cabin itself was almost designed to be hidden in that little gully.

What his old man told him about being lost came back to him. *Don't panic, stay where you are.* People will be looking for you. That's what happens when someone gets lost. They make bad decisions that make things even worse. Blow your whistle, do something to attract attention.

Light a fire!

Plus, he was going to need it. The temperature had noticeably, rapidly dropped, just in the past few minutes. The dark shadows oozing up had an almost physical feel to them, like they were made of tar. There wasn't much time before the light was gone completely.

But how to get wood for the fire? All of the dead wood was buried underneath the thick blanket of snow, and probably soaked from the rain earlier …

The hemlocks!

Underneath the hemlock trees, close to ground level, were typically found dead branches, always dry, sheltered by the canopy above. And the dead hemlock sprigs held enough pine sap to make excellent kindling.

The hemlock boughs on the nearest tree were drooping down, almost touching the ground, fully laden with dollops of snow. He kicked at one of the branches, vibrating enough snow off that the whole branch sprung up like a catapult, levering snow into the air. He twisted around to avoid getting dumped on. Ducking underneath, he saw that inside the cone of the tree, remarkably, only a thin coating covered the pine straw, mostly snowdrift. This would be a good place to shelter, like a natural igloo.

He set the rifle against the trunk, with the nylon strap of the flashlight draped over the barrel so that the flashlight dangled from the stock, providing some light. It was like a cave beneath the hemlock. He started snapping off branches, and quickly realized he couldn't grab well with his left hand. He tried to squeeze some warmth out of the handwarmer, but his fingers jabbed with sharp needle pricks like they had fallen asleep.

He lifted his hand to his face—it also weirdly felt like his arm was full of sand—pressed the cotton glove to his cheek and could feel warmth radiating from the packet. But he couldn't feel the heat in his hand. It had gone numb.

So he worked with one arm, tugging with his whole body to snap off some of the larger dead branches, hunched over the whole time in the confined space. He leaned the larger branches against the trunk of the tree, away from the rifle, and karate-kicked to snap them in two. His left leg, the one that had slipped in the stream, felt like it had drop foot. He wasn't able to lift it well, and so did the jabbing kicks with his right leg.

He tucked the branch fragments under his left armpit. He was still able to squeeze it against his rib to act like a vise and stripped off the smaller branches. He collected them all together and crinkled them up, creating a nest of kindling near the entrance where the boughs had shaken free of the snow. He arranged the larger branch sections in a teepee shape around the ball of tinder.

The box of matches was in his front chest pocket. He had to unwrap the aluminum foil with his teeth, which caused a weird electric shock to run through him every time his enamel touched the foil. He began to shake uncontrollably.

It took a while for the spasm to pass.

The ski glove on his right hand was too thick to handle the tiny box, so he had no choice but to bite a gloved finger and tug it off. The frigid air on his bare hand felt like he'd spilled boiling water on it—a shock of pain and a burning sensation.

He thumbed the box open, awkwardly pivoting the box in his hand so he could pinch out a wooden match. He began to shake again and about half the box of matchsticks scattered free, falling onto the ground and blending in immediately with the pine needles.

Once the bout of shivering passed, he knelt down as close as he could to the kindling, held the matchbox in his teeth with the strike facing outward, and scraped the match across. He smelled the sulfur right beneath his nostrils, one scrape, two scrapes, three. The there was a hiss and the flame burst to life.

He quickly tried to shift the match over to the kindling, but moved too fast and accidentally blew out the match.

Painstakingly, he went through the same motion, extracting another match from the box, losing another bunch again in the process, this time snapping the match because he pressed too hard.

A third try—he held the match at the wrong angle and it burned too fast, the flame running up to his finger, which took a while to register but when it did, his reflexes jerked and he dropped the match.

A fourth try—he got the match to the level of the kindling, but even the dry pine springs were still quite damp and failed to catch on fire.

A fifth try. As he leaned forward in the narrow space, his shoulder bumped against a neighboring bough, dislodged some snow, and caused a mini-avalanche to cascade down on his neck and shoulder and floof on top of the kindling. He dropped the matches too and when he located the box, fumbling around on the ground, it was empty.

By this time the bouts of shaking had become so violent he had to curl up into a ball on the ground.

Then, after a while, the shivering receded, and was replaced by a cozy warmth that spread throughout his body. Like the shots of whiskey at Finn's. All of that shivering must have warmed him up a little.

Need to whistle for help.

He slowly crawled out from underneath the hemlock and struggled to his feet, feeling drunk. Outside it was fully dark, the clouds had rolled through, and now the sky was perfectly clear, an electric blue as the stars appeared, glinting like cold sparks. His breath hung in a sluggish fog around his head.

He felt around inside his jacket for the whistle on the lanyard. *That's strange*, the front of his jacket was unzipped. Ah, right -- he'd opened his coat when he started to overheat back in ... *the Slashings? Hours ago.*

And when he finally located the whistle, it was hard to grasp with his bare hand. *Bare hand?* Damn, he'd forgotten to put his glove back on after the matches. It was back on the ground under the tree, which now seemed very far journey back. He tried to find the other cotton glove in his pockets but soon gave up.

He got the whistle up to his lips and blew three times, as hard as he could. A faint warble came out that he could barely hear himself, like he was at the bottom of the lake, the surrounding hemlocks and deep snow damping the sound, the water of the two streams roaring past.

Who am I kidding? There was no one around. He was lost in The Fortress, and no one hunted in the Fortress. They would not be looking for him here. His tracks had long since been erased by the snow.

From up on the heights came the sound of howling. Coyotes must have found the scent of the buck, bedded high on the ridge above him. Maybe neither of them would make it to see dawn. For some reason, he found that funny.

A sudden wave of exhaustion came over him as he realized he'd been on the go for what—how many hours? He drew a complete blank, unable to do the math. *A long time.*

Nearby an old stump peeked above the snow and Stef flopped down and propped his back up against it.

Rising above the ridgeline were the three bright stars of Orion's belt, to his right the Big Dipper and North Star, and directly above him the big W of Cassiopeia. The blinking lights of an airplane cruised across the clear night sky, five miles up. He pictured the passengers nestled side by side on their way to some big city or warm beach, with no idea whatsoever of the little drama playing out directly below them, or even why it was happening in the first place. And if they knew, they would probably just shake their heads.

Maybe think he had it coming.

No one would ever know about the buck, how close he was to bagging a trophy. Instead, thanks to his kid brother, they would think he had buck fever, dashed off alone into the blizzard, and was dumb enough to get lost.

A cautionary tale: *That year when the Yeager kid froze to death.*

The Milky Way ribboned east to west from horizon to horizon, the stars gleaming so bright they reflected off the fresh snow and provided ambient silver light—enough to see shapes in the landscape.

Something was moving toward him.

A dark shape, slinking forward along the bank of the stream, descending the canyon hollow. The shape split and he saw there were two of them.

Coyotes!

Probably called them in with the stupid whistle. His rifle was way back under the hemlock tree, a marathon distance away. But he had to try.

In his mind's eye, he leaped up, raced across to the opening in the hemlock, slid in, grabbed the rifle, and had it cocked and ready for them when they came for him.

But his legs weren't moving. He was still sitting in the snow, just dreaming all that.

Now they were close, fluid black shapes against the glowing snow. Down at ground level—their level—the coyotes seemed huge. He heard the low growl from the closest, who crept forward toward him, head down, paws forward, ready to pounce. So close, he could see ghostly eyes glittering in the starlight.

The other circled behind him.

So this is it, Stef thought.

He closed his eyes.

He felt pawing at his clothes, tearing at his jacket, his belt buckle, his pants, yanking them off. He wanted to scream but his voice seemed far away. The snow felt soft and silky and warm against his bare skin...

"Wake up!" a voice shouted at him.

He cracked open his eyelids, which took an enormous effort, and met stabbing bright light shining directly in his eyes. There was a dark shadow hovering over him, the light like a burning cyclops in the center of its head.

As if realizing the light was blinding him, a hand reached up, removed the light, and placed it off to the side so the beam was pointed upward.

Skate. Hovering above him.

She took off her blaze-orange tossle cap and her black hair cascaded down around her shoulders. He felt her pull the cap over his head. The backdrop was a soft golden glow all around her

He was in a tent, he dimly realized. The feel on his skin wasn't snow, it was a down sleeping bag, zipped open, and he was lying on top of it.

Fully naked!

Without a word, with a sense of urgency in her eyes, Skate began to undress, unzipping her orange hunting coat, then a fleece sweater, rolling them into a bunch. She sat next to him and crunched her knees up in the air so she could unlace her boots. While in that position, she shimmied out of her snow pants and then her long underwear, revealing the long muscles of her thighs and calves. Then she knelt above him and pulled her thermal top over her head, so that she was naked as well, her long dark hair tousled, her arm tattoos vivid, the swooping eagle in a circle of flames seeming alive, her turquoise necklace dangling between her breasts.

"I ... haven't ever done this before," Stef stammered.

At that, she barked out a laugh.

"One step at a time!" she said, flashing a sharp smile. "First let me keep you from freezing to death."

She switched off the flashlight, climbed into the sleeping bag, zipped it up around them and up over his head and pressed her body tightly against his. Her skin felt like it was on fire.

"Stay with me, Stef," she breathed into his ear.

He silently curled his head into her chest while she cradled him and everything melted into a white-hot haze.

TUESDAY

He woke to the sound of a crackling fire. In a half-dream state, he snuggled deeper into his sleeping bag on the couch at Hilo, with a sense of dread about the upcoming first day of the season that still lay ahead of him.

It took him a few minutes to remember he was in a tent, the yellow domed fabric above him flickering in firelight. It was dark outside. He was alone. And naked.

Skate!

He pictured her and that woke him up fully.

He did not want to leave the warm confines of the sleeping bag, but rolled over, unzipped the tent flap, and peeked outside. Skate was in the process of tossing a dead pine branch onto a bonfire, and a burst of sparks leapt up into the night sky.

She was dressed in her full hunting gear. Had he dreamed her curled up next to him? Then he noticed she was wearing his hat, and that he had on her tossle cap.

All of his clothes hung on a makeshift clothesline formed by two drag ropes lashed together and stretched between a pair of live hemlock boughs, running as close as possible to the flames without the fabric actually catching on fire. His muck boots were speared upside down on a pair of cross country skis jammed upright in the snow, angled so the heat could reach up inside. His gloves dangled like marshmallows from the end of ski poles that were leaned out toward the fire, propped up on Y-branched sticks.

She saw he was awake and brought over his long underwear.

"These are dry."

He tried to shield himself for modesty as he awkwardly wriggled into the bottoms, but she didn't look away, instead knelt down even closer beside the open flap, watching him like a hawk. He followed her eyes to his hands and feet—a mix of bright red, white, and bluish in spots.

"The frostbite isn't too bad," she said. "I think you'll keep your fingers and toes."

One by one she felt a piece of clothing with her bare hands and, once satisfied with its condition, brought it over and passed it to him through the tent flap. Everything was burning hot as he got dressed, though he couldn't tell if the heat was coming from the clothes or his skin, real or an illusion.

Finally he tugged on his boots and crawled groggily out of the tent, standing up in the frigid night air, so cold and dense it felt liquid.

He moved close to the fire. She helped him slip on his hunting coat because his left arm was still stiff.

"Up like this," she said, zipping it all the way, standing close as she did, eye to eye. "Not wide open, like when I found you."

She handed the pair of gloves to him, shaking the right one for emphasis.

"This is the one my dogs brought back to me."

Her dogs?

"I—I thought they were coyotes," he said. "Coming to … well, you know."

"You sure must have been out of it! Gerry and Freddy are twice the size of coyotes." Underneath the hemlock where he had tried to make a fire, he saw the two wolf dogs lying down on the pine straw.

"I didn't know your dogs were named Gerry and Freddy."

"You never asked."

Both of the dogs lifted their heads, hearing their names. They still looked frightening—and hungry—as they stared at him from beneath the pines.

"I had just returned to Thunderbird at twilight and let the dogs out. I'd kept them inside the cabin all day, for exactly that reason, so numbskulls didn't make the same mistake as you and take a shot at them. They were going stir crazy by that point and ran off into the woods …"

She had melted some snow in a tiny metal pot placed right on the coals, and now it was boiling. She fished out a tin cup from her backpack, tore open and emptied a packet of powdered broth inside, filled the mug with hot water, stirred the liquid with a stick.

He took an eager sip, burning his tongue, which made them both smile, Skate shaking her head at him.

"I had just sat down to eat," she continued, "when there was a frantic pawing at the door, the dogs desperate to get in. Gerry had a glove in his mouth, and Freddy was looking back out at the treeline. It didn't take much to put two and two together."

"I had my overnight gear already packed, hanging by the door. Debated on taking it with me in the morning given the forecast, planned on going out past the Fire Tower, but ended up just crossing the grade and hunting the head end of North Fork."

"Any luck?" he asked, almost automatically, hunter's etiquette, like saying please and thank you.

She shook her head.

"I knew there was no way I'd be able to trudge through the deep snow, but I have a pair of touring skis that are made for just these conditions. I put on my heavy ski boots and a headlamp, grabbed the skis and poles, my rifle, and I was out the door. The dogs led me here, about a mile and half, almost all of it downhill, though a little tricky through the woods at night, with just a headlamp lighting the way. Imagine my surprise finding you here lying in the snow."

She added flatly, "Without a minute to spare."

The steaming mug had cooled enough that he could drink. It tasted incredibly good. He felt the thick fog in his head begin to clear.

"So why don't you tell me what happened," she said after a while.

He did his best to retell the events of the day. As he did, he realized the many mistakes he made along the way, embarrassed to say them out loud. But she listened throughout with that even expression of hers, nodding at certain key moments.

By the time he got to the part where he was trying to light the fire, and the matches wouldn't start, the enormity of it all hit him and a wave of emotion rose up and he started to cry.

She came over and held him close, and after a moment in her arms, the wave crested and he began to regain his composure.

"Tell me about the buck again," she said softly.

"It climbed up to this point right above us," he said. "I swear it must still be up there."

She nodded, her hair brushing against his cheek.

"It's almost dawn, Stef. You made it through the long night. I'm going to show you how to get back to the Shawmut Grade. It's not far. They will be looking for you and there will be someone on that road."

She leaned in and whispered, "I'm going to go after it."

He broke her embrace and stepped backward.

"No! I'm the one that has to finish this—" he said, surprising himself at the force of his words.

She sized him up, her blue eyes piercing, trying to determine if he meant it or if this was bravado. He met her gaze and didn't flinch.

"But I'm going to need your help," he added.

Satisfied, she nodded once. "Then let's make a plan."

"But first," she said, and reached out and grabbed him by the wrist. She turned it over, unbuckled the plastic watch, held it up to the light to examine it, before casually tossing it onto the fire. She removed her own and handed it to him. "You need this more than me."

The watch had a stainless steel case, fluorescent dials, a black face, with minute numbers printed around the bezel. In the firelight, he could see a silver crown and the word "Submariner" —all very fancy, except it was attached to an ordinary, sweat-stained band.

"Wear it so the face is on your inner wrist," she instructed. "That way you can check the time without flipping over your elbow, which can look like a tail flick."

"I've never seen a Rolex before," Stef said, ripping and adjusting the fastener.

"From Pops. After my first medal at the World Championships."

"I promise I'll take good care of it," Stef said.

"How about you put it to good use," she smiled. "The time?"

"It's 6:05," Stef read off the glowing dial. "About forty minutes to first light," he added, recalling the timetables.

She took a ski pole and used it like a giant pencil to draw a diagram in a patch of snow they hadn't trampled yet. She sketched a big curvy V, a little lopsided to the right, and jabbed a dot just below the point of the V.

"This is us."

About halfway up the left stem of the V, she placed another dot.

"This is where you last saw the buck," and he agreed.

"I am going to go up the north branch of the Fortress," she traced a parallel line along the left side, "just past where you said you fell in, and then cut up to the ridge." She hooked her line to the right and crossed the V higher up.

"You are going to climb up the needle point right above us." She drew a dash entering the V right at the tip. "These hemlocks run in a line all the way up to the top. Keep in the pines, that should make the climb easier. Less snow. More things to hold onto."

He nodded, trying to push aside doubts about climbing a hill that sounded as steep as a cliff.

"We'll both move in like the pincers of a claw." She drew two lines like arrows coming at the spot that marked the buck, her from the north and him from the south. "If he's there, we'll spring him and have the exits covered."

"Timing is going to be everything," she said. "Otherwise he could slip the noose."

She considered for a moment, then said, "This part of the mountain is at level with the continental divide. Meaning the first rays of the sun will hit up on the heights. The sky is clear. That will be our sign, the sun coming up. That's when we both move."

The fire had died down from the bonfire of earlier to an ordinary fire, and Stef lingered as close to it as he could, watching as Skate made quick work disassembling the campsite.

She dumped the pot and tossed it into the snow to cool, crawled in the tent and rolled the sleeping bag to fit compressed in its pouch, broke down the flexible tent ribs and folded that into another small bag, both of which fit snugly into her backpack.

She retrieved a hand hatchet from among the pines, strapped it along the side of her pack, placed the now-cool pot and his tin cup inside the backpack, and wedged them among the tent and sleeping bag in different spots so there was no chance of them clinking together.

She took down the clothesline and untied the square knot holding the two sections of drag rope together, coiled one and tossed it to Stef, the other went in her pack.

"Gerry! Freddy! Come."

From under the pines, the wolf dogs yawned, stretched out like cats, then stood, loped over, and sat in front of her, expectantly.

"Thunderbird," she said while locking eyes with them. Their ears pricked up.

She held the stare for several seconds, then said with excitement, "Thunderbird! Go!"

And with that, they both leapt into action, bounding away, chasing each other up the middle hollow, leaping across the now-frozen stream, and vanishing into the night.

She ducked underneath the hemlock where the dogs had been laying and retrieved the rifle for him.

"I always wondered where this gun got to," she said, examining the Mohawk closely.

She continued. "I remember when my dad gave it to me. He bought it at a K-mart, it came in this cardboard box with a tomahawk on the side and big red letters 'Mohawk.' My first gun, a birthday gift. Lot of good memories hunting with this …"

She said, "I'm guessing Pops passed it to your dad, when you were old enough. That's how he pays off favors, with things. The old way."

"I had no idea it was yours!" Stef exclaimed, eyes wide. "Do you—do you want it back?"

"No, it's your gun now," she smiled, handing it to him.

Then she stepped even closer, and said, "One more thing."

Stef closed his eyes. *Maybe she was leaning in for a kiss?*

But instead she pulled the tossle cap off his head and replaced it with his own hunting cap.

"I thought I'd keep something of my own, if you don't mind" she said with a wicked smile.

She got her rifle—also sheltered beneath the hemlock—and strapped it to the side of her backpack, then hefted it up onto her shoulders. She adjusted the headlamp over top of her tossle cap. Then she laid the skis side by side on the ground. They were thicker than cross country skis he'd seen before, with metal edges that glinted in the firelight. Her heavy winter boots had a protruding lip in the front shaped like a duckbill, with holes that fit into metal pins when she stepped into the ski bindings, held in place by a bar she clamped down and locked using the tip of a ski pole.

"You are … skiing?" Stef said, incredibly.

"Think of this as the original biathlon." That got a smile from him.

"Seriously, I'll make it there in half the time. Now let's get to it. Good luck, Stef."

"You too, Skate."

And with that, she switched on her headlamp and skied away through the deep snow, leaving a herringbone pattern behind.

The sky had become infused with the slightest tinge of blue, the stars fading, the shapes of the ridgelines solidifying. The glowing second hand made a steady circuit around the watch dial. He knew it was time to get moving, but couldn't pull himself away from the warmth of the fire.

It took the thought of seeing her again to spur him into action.

He walked into the pines, clicking on his flashlight—but immediately saw it wasn't necessary, the ambient light of the snow revealed the landscape in crisp monochrome detail, easy enough to navigate by.

Only twenty yards in, the hillside canted up sharply. A ribbon of hemlocks wound their way up the spine of the hill, tracing the edge of a sheer wall to his right, and transformed into a cascade of icicles emerging from the bare rock. To his left, past the pines, the hillside was sculpted in heavy snow like layers of icing on a cake, looking ready to avalanche if disturbed. But here among the pines, the ground was mostly clear, only a fine layer of frost on the pine straw.

He switched from one tree trunk to the next, slowly but steadily ascending above the valley floor. His left leg was dragging and threatened to slip out from underneath him—his hand shot out to latch on to the nearest tree for balance—and a shovelful of snow fell off the agitated boughs, showering him. Normally he would have brushed it off as an annoyance, but now it struck a minor chord of panic when clumps of snow trickled down the back of his neck.

Before long, he was near the rim. He found a place to stand just below the crest to catch his breath. Far below the tiny orange spark of the campfire glinted. To the southwest, he had an unobstructed view of the horizon, with Orion's Belt setting and the Dog Stars gleaming bright in the cobalt blue sky. To the east, above the lip of the hill, the sky was turning a pale straw color.

He glanced down at her watch. She was right about wearing it reversed, just a subtle twist of the wrist.

7:04. Fifteen minutes. *Not long.*

He was burning hot from the exertion of the climb, but didn't dare unzip anything or remove any article of clothing. And after standing there for just a minute, his body heat dissipated and the biting cold hit him like hammer. His breath crystallized into fine little flakes that hovered around his head. Almost immediately, his toes and fingers started to ache.

A wave of dread swept over him. *What am I doing? Why am I still out here?* Skate had given him an easy out and he should have taken it. *If it weren't by pure chance, right now I would be ...*

He couldn't bring himself to complete the thought.

A shiver ran through him.

Just then, high above, the top of the tallest hemlock at the point of the hill glowed orange, lit up by the first rays of the sun.

Sunrise!

The clouds of doubt vanished. It was time to move.

He unshouldered his rifle and held it at the ready, at chest height. At any moment, the buck could spring up and every fraction of a second would matter. But his left arm ached and almost instantly became fatigued trying to hold the gun in that position, so he let his left arm drop and kept his right cocked at an angle, the barrel pointed down and to the side. *Good enough.*

He crested the hill and could see a narrow triangle of ground dominated by a giant hemlock, easily over five hundred years old—the one that caught the light. He circled around the enormous trunk and beyond, the ground slanting gradually up to the top level.

The snow here on the hilltop was twice as deep, each trudging step forward an effort to break through the icy crust at the surface, only to have his boot plunge down into the deep snow, almost up to the top of his muck boots. In the absolutely still forest, his plodding steps sounded like heavy machinery crushing rocks.

So much for any element of surprise.

He was climbing the final approach to the summit when the full sun rose above the horizon, gleaming off the ice and snow and trees in a kaleidoscope sunburst. He had to turn his head away to avoid being blinded.

When he looked back, the buck was standing there.

In profile with its side presented, silhouetted by the sunrise, head turned backward, looking in the opposite direction, icy smoke wreathed around its head, the sweep of antlers spread wide like two hands cupping the dawn.

Without a moment's hesitation, Stef raised the Mohawk, sighted the bead at the front of the gun barrel at the buck's chest, and fired.

The shot boomed and echoed down the valleys of the Fortress.

When he looked up, the buck was not there. He quickly ejected the shell and reloaded. Then at an almost sprint he crashed up the slope, plowing snow out of the way, looking around wildly to try to catch a glimpse of it moving and get off another shot.

He practically tripped over the buck lying dead in the snow.

It had fallen where it stood, on its side with front and back legs splayed out as if bounding in a final leap. Its right side faced up and there was a thick stripe of crimson blood running down from its shoulder, staining its underbelly—the wound from yesterday. Stef looked at it and could not believe the deer had run miles after that.

It was an enormous deer, easily as long as Stef was tall—and looked like it weighed much more than him. Its neck was thick, an extension of its shoulders, one large mass of muscle.

The antlers were like nothing he'd ever seen on an actual buck in the wild, only mounted up on walls. The curved spread was wide enough to fit completely around his waist. He counted five points rising up like fingers from each beam, and in the middle, two brow tines curved like fangs.

Twelve points!

As he stood there admiring the buck, he could hear crunching footsteps, and turned to see Skate approaching from the north along the edge of the hilltop.

When she got close she said, "I heard the shot."

Stef nodded his head toward the ground and she stopped in her tracks.

"My god."

She walked in a slow circle around the buck, touched the rack, crouched down, and examined the shoulder wound.

"That was a good shot," she said. "Amazing he kept going."

"He was standing here looking back at you. I was just down the slope there. I don't think he ever saw me."

"I crossed his tracks where he sprinted up to the heights, like you said," she said. "And yours, too, wandering around in the valley. I cut up the hill about where you sat down on that log. At the top I stowed the skis, waited, and started moving at sunrise…"

"After a couple hundred yards I came across where it bedded down for the night. A lot of blood, hard to miss. Right where you guessed, on the ridge looking down into the valley. He must have heard me coming from a ways off with this crunchy snow."

They stood there in silence for a minute, the bright rays of the morning sun casting long purple shadows across the hilltop, the snow sparkling like a field of diamonds.

"How are we going to get him out of here?" Stef asked.

She pointed in the direction of the sun. "A straight pull that way. About a mile, out to the Shawmut Grade. We can drag it along the road to Thunderbird. Or if the grade road is driveable, I'll go get my Jeep. But I expect we'll run into people—looking for you."

Stef suddenly became serious.

"Skate, I never told you. Thank you."

She winked. "You'll thank me again later. Now let's get to work."

Skate removed her backpack and placed it flat on the snow a short distance away, took off her hunting coat, folded it in half, draped the jacket partly over the pack, partly on the snow, so they could lay their rifles side by side on top. It was brutally cold—the early sun shining bright but devoid of any warmth—yet she seemed unfazed in just her fleece.

Stef unbuckled the new knife that Doc had given him. He'd seen his old man field dress many deer, but never had done it himself, let alone one this big. Let alone with a woman standing there, watching him.

She helped him orient the buck, flipping it over onto its back with its head uphill on a slight incline, its head lolled off to the side, tongue protruding, two forelegs curled in. Stef spread its back legs and knelt down in the snow between them. He thought about putting on the surgical gloves but felt foolish doing that in front of Skate. She didn't look like she would use gloves.

When he took off his ski gloves, his fingers jabbed in pain. Now in the daylight they looked red and angry, with blotchy white patches near the tips. He was having trouble gripping the knife.

"Do you need help, Stef?" she asked.

He shook his head and adjusted his grip, trying to locate the right place to make the first cut. He pressed, and the knife twisted and slipped out of his hand.

"Stef. You don't have to prove anything," she said, adding, "You already have."

She came over and took the knife from him, hilt first. He stepped back, and she knelt down between the buck's legs. "In the side pocket of my pack there are surgical gloves. Can you get them for me?"

"Here, you can use mine," he said sheepishly.

She worked quickly, cutting a circle around the butthole, then sliced deep around its scrotum and split the crotch down to the pelvis, avoiding the bladder.

Next she walked around and straddled its chest facing backward, and smoothly sliced through the soft white fur at the base of the sternum. She got a grip on the fur, tugging and cutting through the hide as she pulled it away from the abdominal wall, opening up a line all the way down to the pelvis to meet up with the original cut.

She went back to the same starting point, this time working the blade underneath the abdomen, making a little incision that she then slipped two fingers inside, lifting up to pull the lining away from the guts, and then ever so gently slid the knife between the Y of her fingers, unzippering the deer as she worked down its belly, careful not to nick the stomach or intestines as its guts bulged out.

Watching her, Stef realized he wouldn't have been able to make any of these cuts with the shape his hands were in. *Probably would have lost a finger and created another backwoods crisis.*

She sliced around the diaphragm, then walked back to the rear legs, knelt down and reached up underneath the ribs and pulled out the internal organs, which slid down about halfway. She reached further up inside the cavity and severed the windpipe from the inside, and then pulled all the guts free and let them slide away on the snow.

Among the steaming pile, she located the liver and set it aside on the crusty snow, then nicked the sac the heart was in and removed it.

"Come here," she said, and he approached.

She sliced off the tip of the heart and handed it to him.

"Eat this."

At first he hesitated, but saw the look in her eyes and placed it on his tongue. It tasted tangy and metallic. He chewed it slowly as she watched him.

"May I?" she asked, and of course he nodded yes. She cut a strip for herself and together the two of them stood side by side, looking back at the carcass of the buck sprawled out in the snow, silently chewing its heart, swallowing at the same time.

They flipped the buck on its stomach and spread its legs to drain. She folded the surgical gloves in on themselves and tucked them in her pack. From a side pocket, she removed a scrunched plastic shopping bag and used it to wrap up the liver and the heart.

"The tag," she said.

He turned his back to her so she could unbutton his license holder. She handed him the license, golf pencil, and twist tie and he knelt in the snow by the buck's head. He had trouble gripping the tiny pencil and, using his thigh as a writing surface, managed to scribble in the county, the date, time, and number of points on each antler branch, six and six. He ripped the tag along the perforation, handed it to Skate as she cut an incision in the buck's ear and helped attach the tag with the twist tie.

She wiped the knife clean in the snow, dried it against the sleeve of her fleece, then she handed it back to him.

"Doc makes good knives," she said.

While Stef went to find a stick that was long and sturdy enough, Skate crossed the buck's forelegs behind its antlers, cuffed the legs together with rope, continued wrapping several times around the neck and then back through the bound legs. Stef returned with a good branch and she attached the end of the drag rope with a clove hitch. She gave it an experimental tug to make sure everything was secure.

"Are you up to this?" she said, staring him in the eyes.

"Yes. I can do this."

She donned her coat, attached her rifle to her backpack, and hefted it onto her shoulders. Stef wore the strap of the Mohawk crossbody so it wouldn't slip.

"Your skis!" Stef said. They had looked expensive.

"Aren't going anywhere," Skate said. "I'll come back for them later. Now, are you ready? On three."

They both took up the trace and leaned into the wood bar like a pair of sled dogs.

"One ... two ... three!"

On the signal, Stef pushed forward as hard as he could, his legs struggling to find traction in the deep snow. The buck barely moved, its dissipating body heat having already melted and refrozen its fur, sticking to the snow, but they heaved forward again and the body came free and slid forward. Luckily, the surface area of the carcass was spread out and the weight dimpled the snow crust but didn't bust through completely. Otherwise this would be next to impossible.

Now it was a matter of keeping momentum, letting the body slide across the snow, navigating a channel through the trees and around obstacles. A couple times, Stef thought he knew which direction to go and tugged them off course. The buck's body skidded and halted, crunching through the crust and sinking down into the snow. Then it took another surge to get the buck up out of the crevasse and sliding again on the surface.

He quickly learned to just follow Skate's lead.

After a few hundred yards, he was sweating profusely and winded.

"Can we stop for a minute?" he asked breathlessly.

They let the stick drop, and he stood there gasping. He unzipped his coat to cool off, consequences be damned. Skate for her part was calm and composed. He could tell she was sizing him up, wondering if it would be easier to just drag it out herself.

"I can do this," he repeated.

For a fleeting instant he took in the surroundings—the morning sun shining through the bare trees, the deep snow crystalline and reflecting the golden sunbeams and striped purple shadows, the sky overhead now a pure deep blue, not a cloud in sight, everything perfectly still except for his breathing, a cloud of fog with each breath, behind him a trophy buck unlike any he'd ever imagined, and standing next to him, Skate.

"I'm ready," he said.

They got into a good rhythm, moving shoulder to shoulder. Stef concentrated on putting one foot in front of the next, just paying attention a few feet ahead for anything that might trip him up or snag the deer. While his breathing was deep and jagged, hers was even and regular, lungs thrumming in and out like a billows. From time to time, he snuck a glance over at her—her eyes locked in concentration, cheeks flushed, sweat on her brow, hair damp.

He lost track of time.

And then they emerged from the forest onto an open rectangular field, a food plot that sloped down to meet up with the Shawmut Grade. To his left, he could see the square top of the fire tower in the distance, and to the right the road curved away to the west. A black iron gate with the Thiassen logo crossed the road, and for a second he was completely disoriented, before realizing this was the north gate, not the south one he entered a few days ago.

They dragged the buck down to the grade. To his dismay, the road was a ribbon of deep virgin snow-- no signs of tire tracks, footprints, nothing. No one had been this far into the back country since it had snowed.

The idea of dragging the deer all the way to Thunderbird was daunting. He could see Skate shared his concern, puzzling through options.

"In theory the Jeep could make it …" she said, talking to herself. "But then again it could get stuck and then what …"

Stef felt lightheaded, closed his eyes. There was a dull droning buzz in his ears and he feared it was a sign he was about to pass out.

Just what Skate needed, not one but two bodies lying on the side of the road in the middle of nowhere!

Then he realized the sound was not inside his head, it was coming from the distance. *The sound of a motor!*

He looked over at Skate, who also was listening intently.

"Snowmobile," she said.

The sound grew louder and louder and, sure enough, in a few moments a snowmobile appeared around the bend and curved down toward the black gate where they were standing.

Skate nonchalantly raised a hand above her head.

The snowmobile had twin skis in the front, a center track full of packed snow, and was towing a bright red rescue sled fastened by a heavy chain. The Thiassen logo in white was painted on the black glossy hood with Frost Hall in bold lettering underneath. The rider pulled up to the gate and cut the engine, dismounted, and took off his helmet. Stef sort of recognized him. *Maybe one of the guides from Finn's?*

"Heya, Skate!" he said jovially.

"Hey Tim."

"You sure have gone off the grid this time!"

He didn't really pay Stef the time of day, nothing more than shooting him a sideways, mistrustful glance, like *who is this lucky guy?* He didn't seem too surprised, either. Maybe not the first guy Skate had brought out to Thunderbird …

Instead, his eyes were fixed on Skate.

Then, before she could say anything, he noticed the buck in the snow off to the side of road.

"Jesus H. Christ!" he exclaimed. He walked around the gate over to the deer and stood admiring it.

"I'd heard there was a big old buck out this way. Said they saw him out in the food plot here during archery," Tim said, nodding at the snow-covered field. "But I had no idea it was a monster like this. Had I known, I would have brought the high rollers up here yesterday.

Not that they lasted long when the weather rolled in. Most were back around the fire in time for lunch and an afternoon nap—"

"Tim," Skate said firmly, snapping him out of his monologue. "Can you give us a lift back to Frost Hall?"

"Of course!" he said, almost immediately shifting into hired-guide mode, grabbing the buck by an antler and scooting it over onto the rescue sled. "Huh, looks like this old boy was wounded pretty bad yesterday," he observed.

A squawk and hiss and garbled tinny voice came from a walkie talkie in his front chest pocket, which he ignored. But it did spark a thought.

"Hey, craziest thing, I don't know if you heard. Jack Yeager's kid got lost down in South Fork yesterday, hunting up in Frigg's Hollow. They sent me up the grade just in case he showed up over here ... though you'd have to be pretty damn lost to end up way over here."

"That's me," Stef said.

Tim looked over at him, surprised to hear him speak. "Say what?"

"I'm that kid. Stef Yeager."

"And that's the buck he was tracking," Skate said, adding, "And shot."

"Well I'll be damned ..." Tim said, slack jawed for a moment.

Then the thought struck him. "I got to call this in!" Tim exclaimed. "There's a whole army out looking for you, Stef! Every one of the guides and hunters at Frost Hall trucked down to South Fork, game wardens, heck Mr. Thiassen called in everyone."

"And you're the one that rescued us, Tim," Skate said. Tim puffed up his chest a bit at that.

"But now we have to get back to Frost Hall. And radio a doctor. Stef spent the night out here and may have frostbite."

Tim's eyes went wide. "Damn, the thermometer hit minus-five last night. You are one lucky sumbitch."

He called in on the walkie-talkie. "Hey 10-4, this is Tim and I'm out at the North Gate on the grade. I found the Yeager kid! Repeat, I found Stef Yeager. I'm bringing him back to Frost Hall by snowmobile. Need to call in a doctor from town, pronto! Over."

There was a ton of radio chatter that followed, but Stef quickly tuned it out. Exhausted, he went over and climbed onto the snowmobile. There was a gun rack along on the side where he stowed his rifle. Just not having to carry the gun, which had begun to feel like an extension of his body, made him feel weightless. The padded seat under his ass—instead of snow or a wet log or that damn seat cushion—felt incredible.

Tim removed the dragging stick and secured the buck to the rescue sled with nylon straps, then got in front of Stef, turned back, and said, "It's about forty-five minutes back down to Frost Hall. Have to take it slow with the three of us and hauling that big guy behind. It's going to be a little chilly so bundle up, okay? And hold on tight."

He put on his helmet and started up the engine with a thrum. Skate climbed on behind him and nestled up close. Her arms wrapped around his waist as they made a wide U-turn and headed back up the grade.

She leaned her head forward, putting her head on his shoulder, and he felt the warmth radiate out of her as the icy wind rushed past. He slumped back against her and they rocked back and forth and he drifted off to sleep, her strong arms holding him up and keeping him from falling.

◦◦◦

Stef opened his eyes, waking from a long deep nap.

Above him was a high, vaulted ceiling with exposed trusses entirely made of black cherry wood. Two chandeliers, composed of elk antlers arranged in a ring, hung from black iron chains.

Inside! Just the idea that there was a roof over his head.

He was lying on a full-length overstuffed leather couch wrapped in a wool blanket that sported a Native American zig-zag design with vivid orange and electric blue colors. Next to him on a side table was a steaming mug. He sat up and propped the throw pillow he'd been sleeping on behind his back and took a sip—honey, ginger, lemon, and whiskey in hot water.

The couch was positioned before an enormous fireplace of mortared creekstone, with a mounted elk head above a mantlepiece decorated with a Christmas sash of ground pine. A fire was blazing, big blocks of stacked wood with yellow flames leaping high, and glowing orange coals accumulating in a pile below.

A mesh screen was propped in front of the hearth to prevent cinders from scorching the Oriental rug. It was an incredible rug that ran down the center spine of the hall, easily over fifty feet in length. At regular intervals, plush leather armchairs, upholstered loveseats, coffee tables, and reading lamps were arranged in such a manner to allow for intimate conversations, but also plenty of open space for a big group party.

Along the cornice ringing the hall were a series of mounted buck heads with little brass plaques underneath, etched with a name and year. To the right of the fireplace, an arched doorway led out to the entry foyer, and to the left, double doors were propped open, providing a glimpse of the kitchen.

He saw Doc out there, puttering around behind a long wooden kitchen island, wisps of steam rising from a teakettle on the stovetop.

The sides of the hall were floor-to-ceiling windows, with glass doors at the far end that opened out onto a brick patio that had been shoveled and swept clear of snow. A metal fire pit was set up, filled with a mound of white-and-orange coals that had been burning all day.

Beyond the patio, out in the snow-covered lawn by the picnic pavilion, was a metal frame that looked like a swing set without swings. Hanging from the center crossbar were the bodies of four deer—a couple of small bucks, a nice eight point, and then Stef's deer, which dwarfed the others.

A small crowd was gathered around. Stef saw his old man, JR, his uncle, and Mac looking up at the deer, all still in the same hunting clothes they had worn on the first day. For the first time his old man actually looked old—but was smiling. Old Karl Thiassen was there, eccentric as always in a Russian fur cap, smoking a pipe.

And Skate was there, too.

She was in the middle of talking, pointing at the deer, and gesturing with her hands. He realized she was in the middle of retelling the story of how he got the buck.

Just then, through the front windows he saw a vehicle crossing the bridge over North Fork and watched it come up the freshly plowed drive and pull into the front entry circle. The family station wagon.

The driver's side door opened and his mom got out, a worried look on her face. From the passenger's side a doctor from town emerged. Over by the picnic area, JR saw his mom and yelled out, then started running across the yard through the heavy snow toward her.

While everyone was turned toward the new arrivals, Skate looked his way and must have seen him sitting up on the couch, because she smiled and starting walking across the snow back up toward Frost Hall.

Toward him.

ACKNOWLEDGEMENTS

To Dad—you've given me a love of the outdoors

To Mom—you've given me a love of books

To Liz—you've given me love, each and every day

I am forever thankful.